An Irish Mermaid Tale

A Tale of an Immigrant Mermaid

Daniel Thompson

PublishAmerica
Baltimore

© 2009 by Daniel Thompson.
All rights reserved. No part of this book may be reproduced, stored in a retrieval system or transmitted in any form or by any means without the prior written permission of the publishers, except by a reviewer who may quote brief passages in a review to be printed in a newspaper, magazine or journal.

First printing

This is a work of fiction. Names, characters, places, and incidents either are the product of the author's imagination or are used fictitiously. Any resemblance to actual persons, living or dead, events, or locales is entirely coincidental.

PublishAmerica has allowed this work to remain exactly as the author intended, verbatim, without editorial input.

ISBN: 978-1-61546-403-6 (softcover)
ISBN: 978-1-4489-8889-1 (hardcover)
PUBLISHED BY PUBLISHAMERICA, LLLP
www.publishamerica.com
Baltimore

Printed in the United States of America

An Irish Mermaid Tale

A Tale of an Immigrant Mermaid

Introduction

At the dawn of the 18th century, social and religious pressure had the Scot-Irish people withdrawn to immigrant ships in the port of their native land. They were perched in County Antrim at the port of Belfast, prepared to march onto the last gang plank to colonial America. They thought that they would be free of the persecution and oppression that they had known in their homeland.

England's intentions of taming the independent minded Irish or eliminate their culture were finally producing results Efforts over the last one hundred and fifty years to implant more obedient English and Lowland Scottish families had failed miserably but the devastation of their fragile economy was finally having the desired result.

The potato famines of 1720 through 1740 eliminated their ability to feed themselves. The famine pushed them to the ports where they were packed on ships to a land where they had been told they could live in peace.

The Scot-Irish immigration to America was in full swing by 1720. The vision of America as a land of infinite opportunity was being was being publicized at home. Owning land was not a reality that the Irish had ever known or a dream that they ever considered real. Under English rule, a family's value was determined by bloodline. In America, wealth and worth were to be measured by the land that a person had cleared, made productive and passed on to future generations.

The possibility that a man could own and profit from his own labor was not a possibility to the Scot-Irish, and therefore never grew roots to the independent minded Irish.

Fishing traditional villages of the northern Irish coast lived remote existence where nature influenced their lives above all things. Much of their understanding of the natural forces was drawn through interpretation of supernatural Irish legends of the sea including the lore of Irish Mur'uchs, Merrows and Selkies.

Events in the small fishing village of Ballyhalbert and around the Ard Peninsula were seen through these legends. Fishermen often disappeared. Their failure to return was believed to be a result of intervention of the supernatural forces of Mur'uchs.

Chapter I

William O'Donovan worked his trawling nets beneath the familiar surface of the deep waters far from the shore of the remote fishing village of Ballyhalbert on the Irish, Ard Peninsula. The racket from circling gulls led William to schools of herring below. The loud clattering and screeching of circling gulls filled the air with their anticipation of the harvest to come. As William retrieved his nets, they dove to the surface and helped themselves to their share of the rolling ball of netted herring. Without the clamber of feeding birds above the surface, the school of herring would be missed. "The sea provides, and the sea takes," as the village elder would say.

William was among the few peninsula fishermen who operated a boat large enough to reach deeper waters of the North Irish Sea where the annual herring migration passed the village.

During the herring season, William brought in large loads of herring for which he reaped a substantial profit from the markets of Belfast. A boat like William's depended on a predictable income brought by an experienced fisherman. The lenders who financed William's boat demanded a profitable return on their investment, including a share of the income from the herring harvest. Herring migration time was a fortnight long peak of fishing and earning season.

In recent decades herring stayed out, away from the shore near the village. William reaped the benefit of his larger boat during the annual cycle of migrating herring as it brought them through the North Irish Sea between Ballyhalbert and the Isle of Man. In the past, fisherman worked near the shore. Generations of burning kelp and dumping garbage near the herring bays eliminated that opportunity.

Old timers recalled stories of locals sharing the wealth of herring season. Such profit was no longer to be had by those who could not work the waters beyond sight of the village. They had no choice but to stand near the pier on Shore Street and wait for William to return at the end of the day.

William's catch began to fill barrels that he used to stow the catch. During herring migration the barrels would be filled and the floor of his skiff would struggle to hold the remainder. He and his crew worked long, difficult hours during the season. There were too few days in the year when herring migration brought them into the waters between Ballyhalbert and the Isle of Man. William needed to match this opportunity with special effort if he was to collect what was expected of him. He was determined to work as fast as he could and load his boat with thousands of kilos of herring over the next few days. He demanded the most from his nets, boat and the crewmen who tracked the boat over the schools of herring.

In other seasons, plaice, cod and haddock filled those barrels. These common fish did not provide the profit that herring brought, but they secured a good living for William. He took the off season catch to his market, where his wife Sarah, ran the store. The remaining fish went to the waiting locals.

Sarah began her work routine when William returned to the pier with his catch. Cod and plaice were offloaded onto a boat from the Belfast market. It arrived in the late morning to coincide with William's return to the Ballyhalbert pier. Market operators in Belfast depended on boats like William's to supply a fresh daily catch of high quality fish.

The leftover catch of odd species was sold to villagers from Sarah's market stand. Any remaining fish would be taken home and prepared for William's dinner or given to the local public house where it would be prepared and served for the evening's supper. These tasks filled William and Sarah's daily routine and provided sufficient income for their lives in their remote village.

The oarsmen moved the boat in a practiced pattern as William retrieved the net from his position at the stern of the boat. The net came over the transom and ran up, onto a large spool that collected the net and prepared it for the next pass over the schooling fish. Herring dropped to the floor at William's feet as it came over the transom. William worked quickly, anticipating the next pass. The faster he retrieved his net and unloaded its contents, the faster he would release the net on the spool to collect the next load. The circling terns and gulls marked the location of herring schools as they moved along. William's crew moved the boat in the direction of the migrating fish and the feasting birds that followed them.

The life of a fisherman in Ballyhalbert was a time honored occupation. One day followed another, with few interruptions from the tedium of the age old methods of casting out nets and retrieving them with the catch snared within. William's boat followed this routine every day except Sunday.

Story telling at the local pub filled the void of news in remote Ballyhalbert. Sea legend and lore were the foundations of many stories as events in Ballyhalbert tended to be explained through interpretation of sea lore and its influence on daily life.

William began to retrieve his nets for the last time of the day when he observed something unusual. A strange ripple appeared on the surface near the stern of the boat. He tied off his net to take a better look at what was causing this disturbance.

"What was it?" one of the oarsmen asked.

"Seals," William answered. He resumed his net tending. The he got a glimpse of the creature that caused the disturbance on the surface. His eyes fixed on the creature, swimming easily, gracefully along side the boat. The light above the creature was poor. The creature was on the darker side of the boat, making it difficult to see many details. William's trained eyes told him that he saw a long graceful creature with a slender body and a large, fish like tail. His mind resisted that conclusion, for there was only one creature that matched what William's experience eyes told him.

Trying to fill the awkward silence, he repeated, "Must be the seals." William knew all of the types of fish and mammals that frequented these waters and he was fully aware that this was not a seal. All sea creatures of this region had behavior patterns that were familiar to William. He also knew that seals seldom traveled this far out from the village harbor. He had fished these waters for over thirty years and had seen most of what the North Irish Sea had to offer. He knew that the sounds and sight of the ripples on the otherwise calm surface were not caused by seals but he dared not speak of his conclusion.

He shook his head and continued to retrieve his net when he saw dark, flowing hair that extended down the creature's back. It swam along beside the boat with a slight and smooth movement of its long powerful tail. Then it darted about in turns and rolls like a frolicking seal.

William saw long, graceful arms and hands extended over the creatures head as it playfully rolled and darted about William's boat. It moved with quick flicks of its tail and rolled onto its back near the surface. William saw the creature's face and upper body for the first time. "Oh my God!" William uttered. "Oh my God. Not now," William uttered quietly.

The crewmen dropped their oars and joined William at the stern to get a view of what their captain had seen.

"I don't see anything. Must be seals, or the birds," the other said. They returned to their oars.

William emptied the content of the net on the floor. He kept his eyes on the water's surface as his oarsmen moved the boat towards the herring, marked by the circling gulls.

The creature surfaced twice more, rolling near the surface before it disappeared under the glare of the morning sun. It unmistakably revealed the graceful creature that caused the surface ripples. William saw the long purple and green dorsal fin that extended down its graceful back to the round, female rump that was revealed, as if intentionally above the surface. Graceful arms moved gently along the creature's side as it arched its back and slowly stroked its tail, moving it along with the appearance of little effort. It followed the boat, swimming on its back, just below the smooth surface. The face, chest and belly of hauntingly beautiful were clearly visible. She was stunning.

William knew the Irish lore of sea maidens. Such tales were spoken of frequently among the men at Ned's pub. They were part of Irish lore that had existed in this region for centuries. Most believed that the tales originated in the cold sub arctic waters of the Baltic in Norway and were brought to Ireland and Scotland by Viking crews in the first few centuries. The Vikings had intermarried with the old Celtic people on the coasts of Caledonia and Hibernia and they brought their sea legends with them. The stories became part of the original Pictish people of Scotland and the Scotti of Ireland under the ancient and combined reign of the Kings of Dalriada. Such legends helped those who lived near the sea explain the forces of nature in their remote existence and the mysterious disappearances of their fellow villagers.

William knew that there was only one creature that fit the description that his eyes registered and his mind denied and he knew that she was part of those ancient traditions. There were no other possibilities. This beautiful creature was the fabled Mur'uch of the North Irish Sea. Some called them Mermaids, or Maidens of the Sea, but in Irish lore they were referred to as Mur'uchs, Merrows and Selkies.

By staying within view of the village, they forced locals to learn to live with them in their midst. They were a part of life by the sea.

Irish Sea lore told the tales of Mur'uchs since the time of Roman occupation of northeastern Ireland and western Scotland. The Mur'uch was said to be hauntingly beautiful and dangerously alluring creature of the sea. They taunted fishermen and seamen who took their living from the waters of her domain.

"William," one of the crewmen said "what is it now? Have you gone daft, man?"

"No! Certainly not," William growled. "Mind your oars," he growled.

As they made their way through the harbor entrance and began to cross the harbor, William's eyes focused on the customary crowd of seals sitting on the moss covered rocks that marked the entrance to the harbor. They were swimming around the rocks as they frequently did in noisy anticipation of a meal of fish parts from Sarah's market.

William turned his attention to his duties of preparing the boat for docking while he tried to ignore the creature that captured his attention this morning when his mind he recalled the details of one of the creatures on the rocks. He looked back straight at a creature that he recognized immediately.

"No," he mumbled. "I knew it. Why now?"

Old timers frequently talked about Mur'uchs, Selkies and Merrows in the village pub. Some fisherman of William's generation dismissed such talk as old man's chatter and wives' tales. Irish lore told of seamen who followed hauntingly beautiful creatures to sea. Their minds were held captive by her beauty and the lure of her song. William did not deny their existence. He had seen Mur'uchs in the area before. He knew that there was no denying their existence.

Irish legend told tales of sailors who chased Mur'uchs onto the sea, often disappearing into the depths of the Irish Sea, never to be heard from again. She took from their numbers just as fishermen took fish from her domain. It was understood as the natural cycle of dependency of all creatures that dwell near the sea.

Old timers talked about several different Mur'uchs that had been seen over the years on or near the Ard Peninsula. Some were said to have long blond hair, while others had black, silky hair. Regardless of their hue, it flowed down the creature's backs to the base of their hips and shapely rumps. While they described the vision of their own experience of blond or black hair, there was one other feature that never varied. They all had large, black eyes like those of a seal pup. Dark and deep, they wept.

A Mur'uch's eyes are as alluring as her song. Men who looked into them were said to lose a hold of their mortal lives and forsake all when they became entrapped by her power. Many followed these maidens into the sea. Tales of missing fishermen existed in every village of the peninsula of northern Ireland. The local pub kept a placque on the wall with the names of fishermen who met their end at sea. There were no markers in the local cemetery for these men. Their remembrance came with the pub wall.

William's beautiful maiden held his eyes. Unashamed of her nakedness or his unrelenting gaze, she looked back at him and smiled. She was aware of his inability to look away. Her black eyes held his vision as if his head had been strapped in a guillotine, unable to escape the inevitable tragedy that she brought to her victims.

"Oh, my God!" he repeated. William's crewmen did not respond. They looked at each other and shrugged their shoulders.

William's mind was fixed on the form of the beautiful sea creature sitting among the seals. Her long, graceful, fish like tail bent at her knees and ended in a large, graceful fluke. Her upper body was smooth, without the scales on her lower body. She had long, coal black hair that came over her shoulders, partially hiding the breasts of a mortal woman peering through the long silky strands. She wore sea lilies in her hair. Kelp adorned her shoulders like a fur boa of a London lady of class. Her eyes teased William to look away, playing innocent, like a lady caught bathing nude on a summer shore.

She abruptly changed her mood to a sultry maiden. She shook her head to adjust her hair. She arched her back and her hair fell back over her shoulders, exposing her breasts for William to see. She unabashedly displayed her form, turning her torso so that she was silhouetted in the mid day sun. The light glistened on the drops of sea water that momentarily clung to her face and then dropped, sensuously on her breasts and then onto her lap. She shook her head once more, her chin lifted high in the radiance of the warm, midday sun.

"Oh my God!" he said quietly. William remembered some of the tales of mermaids from the eastern coast of Ireland. William was familiar with the features of several maidens that were known to exist off of the rocky shores. William was sure that this one was different. She was different than the others who he recalled. Since Mur'uchs were jealously protective and territorial, not known for moving out of their native territory, William wondered how this one had taken possession of the rocks near Ballyhalbert. William could not recall tales of this particular beauty. "She is new to this region," he reasoned.

She held his gaze. He could not look away. She peered through William's eyes, into his mind for his personal critique and preferences for the details of her body.

Her form changed again, adopting the preferences of his mind. She took the slim form of a young woman with a narrow waist and flat belly. Her upturned breasts stood firmly, proudly upon her chest.

William felt the throttle of her hold on his gaze. He was unable to turn away. Astounded by her ability to know his mind and the details of his imagined ideal female form, William was dazed and light headed. He stumbled backwards and covered his eyes, but her hold was firm and unyielding. William was not released until she sensed his approval. A smile crossed her soft lips and then a kiss came from her lips and her hand when she saw that she fulfilled his every preference for the ideal beauty.

Her hair held traces of blue hue in the radiance of the sun. Her big, black eyes appeared wet and deep. Her narrow waist separated the form of a powerful sea creature from the bust and shoulders of a human female. Her hips were broad and the white belly was soft and inviting to his eyes. The supple round shape of her backside produced an involuntary, but pleasant vision of lying with her.

She shifted her position, her arms moved to support her from behind. She moved her knees from side to side, her legs bent like a shy school girl sitting under a shade tree. The lustful images that she brought to his mind were strong and inescapable. William uttered, "She was perfect."

The ideal of beauty, sensuality and lust that a man has for the perfect woman sat before him.

She took pleasure in revealing herself to William. She cupped a breast in her hand while she stretched and arched her back. William was drained, light headed and alarmed by her bold display and his inability to control his mind or his private thoughts.

"Enough," he mumbled. His mind was wracked with sensual visions and he was drained by trying to avoid her hold on him. She turned away. She slowly revealed the rounded flesh of her half naked rump before she slipped off of her rock and into the sea. Mercifully, she disappeared under the surface and out of sight.

William and his crew remained silent when they reached the pier and tethered the boat to the ancient iron rings fixed to the old sea wall. William was not sure what his oarsmen saw of the Mur'uch. He was far too spent to think of it any further. He needed to collect himself before he met Sarah at the market.

The crew hoisted the barrels up onto the pier where workers took them away. William followed them and greeted Sarah when he arrived at the market. She separated the catch to be sold in the local market from that which would be sold in her local market. She began to arrange her fish display for customers who waited impatiently for a view of what she had to offer today. The catch of haddock and cod filled baskets on her counter.

She collected a filets of plaice and cod for delivery to Ned's pub as she did nearly everyday.

William always supplied fish for villagers. Those that needed fish but could not pay were given a share. Sarah never turned anyone away if she had fish to give. Ballyhalbert was small and its families had lived together in this region for many generations. They all suffered and prospered with the give and take of the sea's bounty. No one person or family owned the sea or its bounty. The catch was shared by all as a sign of Ballyhalbert.

William remained nervous, even after he met Sarah at the market. His hands shook from his battered nerves. He tried to conceal his agitation, but it was no use. Sarah's knowledge and intuition saw through his transparent attempt at disguising his jumbled nerves. Villagers of Ballyhalbert knew the life of a fisherman and the dangers that they faced every day. Sarah and the other women were familiar with the forces of the sea that played out in their lives and the forces that played on local fisherman.

Sarah also knew of the tales of Mur'uchs and Merrows as well as the Selkies that lived among them although women seldom spoke of these matters in public. They saved their observations for quieter times when they could speak among themselves. They met this reality with the silent strength that came from the knowledge that they were powerless to change the supernatural influences in their lives.

"You are upset, William, what is it?" she asked. "Were the seas rough this morning?"

"It is nothing," William said. "I am just tired. The herring season tires me more than it did when we were young." The smile that he created to cover his state of mind disappeared as quickly as it began.

Nothing further was said. Sarah did not push her husband on the matter as she unloaded his barrels and began selling the day's catch. A crowd surrounded Sarah's market. They began to claim the harvest that William and his crew provided.

The following day, William and his crew were back on the herring fishing grounds. William resisted looking out onto the sea or along the boat for fear that the Mur'uch would return. He resisted the pleasure of recalling her beauty. Unable to keep her from his mind, William remained silent.

They returned to shore in the late morning and delivered their catch to Sarah. William had not seen the sea maiden. Sarah said nothing about the change of his mood. She let him be and busied herself with her chores.

The following day, it appeared that William would not refresh his lust filled mental vision of his mermaid. When the boat returned to harbor, he caught sight of her sitting among the seals where she had been before, amusing her self with their play. She was as stunningly beautiful, just as his memory recalled. She sat, perched upon her rock, her long, silken hair danced seductively below the arch of her lower back and her round backside.

She smiled at William, as if to tease him with the possibility that his crewmen would see him in his disturbed mental state. William and the crew went on to the pier and finished their day. He was too wrecked to say much to anyone. He was unable to sleep or turn his attention to anything, or anyone while the Mur'uch took possession of his mind.

William visited Ned's Pub on Back Street. He ordered a whisky to calm his mind and restless hands. As customary, William was greeted by his friends and neighbors. O'Malley, the village elder and resident patron of Ned's pub sat in his rocker, closest to the peat lit fireplace, waiting on someone to buy him a drink. A pipe in his hand and an empty glass beside him, he looked at William with anticipation. William ordered a whisky from the bar and brought it to O'Malley.

"Here ya' go, old timer," William said. "Enjoy."

O'Malley had been a fisherman in this region for many years. He was much too old to face the daily challenges of a fisherman. Instead, he sat in his rocker and watched. The smoke from his old briar pipe rose and mingled with the smell of fried cod, cabbage and potatoes coming from the stove in the back of the pub and the warm earthy smell of the peat fire in front of him.

The old rocking chair was understood to be O'Malley's, as it had been for other senior village story tellers of previous generations. No one ever took his place by the fire. It was a place of honor for the old sage who sat in it as if presiding over a solemn rite of passage.

O'Malley saw the disturbed expression of William's eyes. It showed the uneasiness of a veteran fisherman who had made a living on these waters for many years. Few things would have produced the torment O'Malley saw on William's face. He recognized it immediately.

O'Malley knew that William had seen something that deeply disturbed him. He knew all of the tales and the lore of the North Irish Sea on the shores of northeastern Ireland and the Scottish coast. With this knowledge, O'Malley looked upon one of Ballyhalbert's senior fishermen. Time would reveal what troubled William.

Several days went by without William seeing his mermaid. He began to find some relief from her absence. He had been tormented by her image and the memory of her siren song. He appreciated the opportunity to be relieved of it and prayed that she would stay away.

Over the last few days he reflected on his abundant life with Sarah. She was, by far, the most beautiful woman in the village and she brought in a respectable income from her market. They had a beautiful daughter together and he was certainly not interested in another woman. He would be pleased to remain with her.

Several days later, William's boat entered the harbor and prepared to approach the pier. He saw the Mur'uch sitting upon her rock. She was wearing a dark gown that draped the full length of her body, from her shoulders to the rock that she stood on. The draping fabric loosely covered her nude body beneath it. As William's boat neared, she stood and waved. William nervously looked around to see if his crew saw her.

The front of her gown was unbuttoned, revealing the naked beauty within.

William was fully enchanted with this maiden and he sensed that he had been moved beyond the point of his control or his ability to escape her power. Over the fortnight since he had first seen her, he had been unable to leave the thought of her behind despite his contentment with Sarah. He was trapped in the vision of her. He had fought against the notion of trying to catch her, but he knew that she held him and he knew the consequences that his actions would bring. The outcome for a seaman unable to escape the power of a Mur'uch had been known for many, many generations of Ard fishermen.

One late evening, O'Malley called William to his side. O'Malley sat in his customary place by the fire.

"William," he said, "you must fight against the powers of this creature. She will have you if you cannot find it within you to resist her."

William said nothing. He stared into the fire and then at his feet as he sat beside the old timer.

"William, let her go. You will be among those who perish in the darkness of her domain," O'Malley pleaded to William's silence. "You will never have her. William, she will take you under and you will never experience the satisfaction of the lust that you have for her."

"It is not in my control, Old Timer," William said. He rose from his seat beside O'Malley and placed a hand on the old man's shoulder. "I have lived in this region for many years, as have my family, before me. My soul is in the water of these shores. I take from it and now it will take me in return."

William had been tormented by the maiden's memory, day and night. He could stand it no longer, even though he knew how his end would come. He walked from the pub to the pier and took the dinghy out among the rocks to find her.

Sarah knew the end that faced William. She knew the consequences that came when a mortal was captured by a Mur'uch. She knew it better than any in Ballyhalbert and she met that knowledge with silence.

Several nights went by before William saw his mermaid sitting on her rocks, brushing her hair. As he neared her, she glared at him to warn him away. She held her hand up to stop his approach.

"Do not approach fisherman! You will never know this world again if you come closer. I am of the sea and if you choose to approach my domain, you will become part of it as well," she warned.

William stopped, alarmed momentarily by her scorn and the sound of the raspy voice that came from deep within her soul. He had not heard her speak in this manner. Her words came from deep within her chest. It sounded as if were in a dream.

Her open mouth revealed the jagged teeth of a predatory fish and the saliva that stretched between her upper and lower jaws. With her hand raised, she roared, "Go back fisherman! William covered his ears from the roar and screech of the sea monster's voice.

"I will not live in your world and I will not relinquish my powers to you and be taken ashore as your tamed woman. Be warned that I will bring an end to your life among mortals, she roared." William moved towards her, unable to regain control of his body or his mind.

The monster stood over him, lowering her massive head close to his face as it blasted him with its warnings. He stood unaffected by her attack.

Seeing his hopelessly entranced state of mind, the creature returned to its sea maiden form and let him approach. "Be it as you make it, fisherman. Come to me then," she commanded.

William stepped out of his boat and climbed the rock to stand near her. She sensed an objection in his mind and backed away, scattering the seals that had gathered around her.

She was puzzled with William's gaze upon her. She sensed that he saw something that did not fulfill his final fantasy. She held up her hand and blocked his approach.

"What is it, fisherman?" she asked.

She gathered her hair over her head with her hands held high so that his view was unobstructed. His eyes followed her naked form from her long, sensuous legs that traced below the scaled skin of her lower body to her rounded buttocks.

"Kiss me then, fisherman," she commanded. "See if my embrace will satisfy your wanting and calm the aching for me. Feel the warmth of my kiss. Caress that which you hold in your eyes. See if I am not the perfect vision of you imagination. My belly is soft and milky white, like my bottom," she said as she led his eyes, examining every detail of her form.

William eyes fixed upon her perfectly shaped bosom. They stood out firmly on her chest and in his caress as he palmed one in his hand. He kissed her lips as she commanded. He gave in to her demands and met the firmness of her lips and the hunger of her passionate embrace.

The surprising warmth of her wet body took him beyond return to his world. She held him close. Her face was as warm as the shallows of the shore on a hot mid summer day. Her face was as wet as if she stood out in the rain, with her face up, to catch rain drops like a child. She tasted sweet, like fresh scallops, raw and delicate in their natural state.

When she released her hungry embrace, his stare stayed fixed upon the milky white mounds of her breast still cupped in his hand. It was soft, full and heavy in his hand. She permitted him this pleasure like few mortal women would allow. She showed enjoyment from his touch and investigation of her soft flesh.

"Do you allow me this pleasure so easily?" he asked. "Your skin is soft and the curves of your body are all that a man could desire, and yet you let me enjoy this closeness and the caress of my appreciating eyes and hands."

Still, she sensed an objection. "What is it fisherman? Do you lust for something more?" she asked. "Shall I change something more to your liking? Tell me what it is that keeps your approval from me. Am I not the picture of your desire?" she whispered near his ear.

"Yes!" he stuttered with all of the courage that he could muster. "You are flawless," he lied.

"Ah! I see what it is. Why did you not tell me what I lacked? This is your end time fisherman. Your mind's eye must be satisfied with my allure."

"Now I know what you saw lacking," she said.

She stooped down and collected two empty sea shells from the rock. She smiled knowingly and placed one high on the breast still cupped in his hand. He held on to her and leaned back to allow her to place the remaining shell on her other breast where her natural nipple would have been.

Before his unrelenting stare, the shells began to change form. They absorbed into her white flesh, leaving the dark, raised nipples as he had envisioned.

"You can read my mind," he said.

"Now you are true perfection," he uttered

"Yes. It is all right fisherman," she said. "I see what you saw missing. I have never needed nipples before. Do you like them?" she playfully asked, lifting the other breast for his close inspection.

"If that will be all, may we go?" she asked.

He held her closely, not wanting to let her go, even for a moment. His passion to possess her was all consuming.

"Follow me and I will bring you the peak of pleasure that you have imagined since you first saw me."

William returned to his dinghy and absentmindedly followed her out of the harbor and onto the open sea. She raised her hand when they were out of view of the village. William stopped rowing and stowed the oars. She slid up onto the boat and the bench before him. Her body glistened in the warm moonlight. Water dripped from her sleek, wet hair, down between her breasts and onto her lap.

"Come to me," she whispered. He stood and she began to take his coat, pants and shirt from him.

"Come to me fisherman," she said. She leaned back onto the seat and pulled him onto her belly easily as if he were a small child. He buried his face in the smell of the sea that came from her hair and the silky smoothness of her shoulders and neck.

He took one of her wet breasts in his hand and playfully thumbed the new creation that sat proudly upon it. She giggled like a newly wed as he began to caress her shoulders and then down upon her soft belly. She moved his hands around to her rump. She placed her hands on his butt and held him against her with more strength than William found comfortable. He tried to shift his body but was unable to move in her hold.

She held him captive as she rolled over the side of the dinghy and into the sea, taking William with her. He had the momentary sensation of her wrapping her legs around his butt, holding him in as they sank deep into her domain.

William never returned to consciousness. His last thoughts, as he met her thrusting rhythm, were visions of his life fleeting away. It briefly occurred to him that he always knew how he would meet his end at sea. He intended to become part of the legend of Irish Merrows, Selkies and Mur'uchs. Now he would become part of the lore of Ballyhalbert. His consciousness slipped away as she sucked air from his mouth with her kiss. She took William deep, into her realm. He resisted her hold on him no longer.

Days later, William's crew told Sarah that they had found the dinghy, without William. They did not tell her that his clothes were found on the boat.

Sarah stayed in Ballyhalbert for several months following William's disappearance. William's crew continued to work the boat and bring the catch to her. She shared the profits with them and they were happy with the temporary agreement. After a couple of months she sold the boat to them.

By Spring, the money that she received from the sale of the fishing boat, fishing equipment and dinghy was gone. The last thing that she did before leaving Ballyhalbert was to sell her fish market. It was enough to set her free from the hold of Ballyhalbert and allow her to attend to her one last need. She could now put all of her effort to raising her daughter.

Sarah did not need to be told what had happened to William. Irish folk lore had the answer to that question and so did she. William had found a Mur'uch and joined her beneath the sea. She knew this tale well and so did many of the villagers. The sea had taken him as it had many others.

The Mur'uch who took William to the depths of the sea was not the first mermaid that he had encountered. Sarah had come to Ballyhalbert's shores many years before and sat upon the rocks at the entrance to the harbor. She lured William to her rock.

William had taken her purple and seal skin hat and hidden it from her. As lore said, he had kept the hat from her during the years that they lived together. As long as he kept it hidden, she would stay with him in his world as a mortal wife.

Sarah had kept a secret from him as well. She had called William's Mur'uch to Ballyhalbert to take him into her embrace and the depths of the North Irish Sea. Sarah's need to care for her daughter was much stronger than her attachment to a mortal husband.

William had treated Sarah well and had given her a beautiful, raven haired child. William had been good to both of them, but Sarah intended to see her to a better life, away from the poverty of William's remote fishing village. Sarah had no intention to stay in the poverty of this village and her one room hut. She and her daughter were destined for more in life.

Even though William was kind and good to Sarah and their daughter, he had held her captive in his mortal world and Ballyhalbert. Their lives were as comfortable as anyone's in the village but she had longed for her return to her own realm.

William and Sarah both knew that if she ever found her hat, that she would slip back into the sea and resume her life as an immortal. The tie between Sarah and William would then be released as told by the legend. Her hat held her immortal power. When she claimed it from William's trunk where she had found it months before, she knew that she could return to the underworld as she wished. Sarah developed her plan for William's end, and the end of her captivity in Ballyhalbert.

She cared for her daughter in the way of Irish Mur'uchs. Legend held that they were caring and loving mothers. Their gift was their love of children. Sarah would have been forced to live out her life with William had she not found her hat in an old trunk before his planned disappearance.

Sarah put the hat away with her other belongings for safe keeping. She would pass it on to her daughter someday, when the time was right.

Chapter II

The cobbled street and stone sea wall marked Shore Street in Ballyhalbert. The age old pier was accessed by use of an ancient iron ladder bored into the stone on the face of the sea wall. The ladder led to tethered boats lined along a narrow pier. The ancient channel gave fishermen access to the small, unprotected harbor and onto the open sea. Surviving fishermen of Ballyhalbert were veterans of stepping down the ladder and finding their boat in the dense fog of the early morning. They knew the course through the old harbor. Sight was much less vital than the senses of their memories that escorted them through their daily tasks.

In the beginning, the tiny town paid its taxes and tithes to the Benedictine Priory of St. Andrews of the Ards from income of its fishery. Locals of centuries ago knew St. Andrews as The black abbey for the black, hooded garment worn by its monks who came to collect from locals who seldom used currency. Monks were sent on their way with a basket of fish and a jug of malt whisky.

In William's time, little was left of the priory that might remind the people of its beginning in twelfth century. Locals dismantled the abbey and used the stones to build or refurbish their own dwellings over the past two hundred years of modern times. Henry VIII found that trying to collect from Ballyhalbert was like squeezing blood from the very rocks that these stoic Ard people called home.

Ancient Nordic ways and lore of the sea were so engrained into the daily lives of Ballyhalbert locals that few knew that their roots led to a time long ago in Norway. The legends of the sea and those who lived beside it made the people of Ballyhalbert as much a part of the sea as the fish within. Ballyhalbert's people depended on the fish that were brought ashore by local fishermen. When the fishing failed to supply their needs they looked for explanations through sea legends and lore.

The local public house was the center of their lives in the small village. It operated as an extension of their one room homes. Most evening meals were taken in the pub after William's catch was prepared by Ned McTavish and his family.

There was little mourning for William except for what Sarah was expected to do in public for the benefit of their daughter. The events of sea maidens and fishermen were all part of an ancient and perpetual legend of joining a mortal man as a loving wife, and raising children before returning to their own world. The people of Ballyhalbert knew the cycle of the give and take of the North Irish Sea, and the opposite realms of Mur'uchs and mortals.

Sarah's daughter had her mother's large dark eyes and shiny black hair. When she was able to take her daughter away from this barren village and to the promise of a better life, she planned to move to Belfast. She would then slip back into the sea and resume her place as the all powerful Queen Maiden of the North Irish Sea.

Children of sea maidens possessed some of their mother's powers. Some held more than others, but they all had the power to manipulate their way among mortals.

Ballyhalbert had several dark haired adults and children. They were well known in the region for their power and their deep mood swings. Sometimes they were the most joyous people of the village and sometimes they were sullen and reclusive. Villagers recognized their special powers and avoided speaking of them.

There were tales of the "Black Irish" from this region. Some confused them with the children of mermaids. The Black Irish were descendants of sailors from the Spanish Armadas who came ashore after ship wrecks in the North Irish Sea. While they too had dark eyes and black hair, they did not possess the powers of Mur'uch.

There was no mistaking Sarah's influence over all things of the sea.

Sarah had overseen the annual Spring festival. It marked the end of winter and the beginning of the fishing season. During festival, village fishing boats paraded over traditional fishing grounds. The village priest blessed the village and the fishing grounds and gave thanks for their past bounty.

They would not have entrusted this important rite to anyone other than Sarah. She was considered a part of the forces that controlled the fortunes of the people of Ballyhalbert. The old timers knew Sarah's moods well. When Sarah was in a good mood, the village prospered. When she was sullen, storms and tragedy could be expected to fall on Ballyhalbert. Before each Candlemas season, villagers did all that was within their ability to keep Sarah happy. She was not one to be encountered lightly.

No one spoke, outright, about Sarah's influence over the forces of nature. Like many forces of Irish legend, she was accepted in the community without explanation.

Sarah and her daughter moved to Belfast following the Spring Festival. Despite the economic problems of the city, they lived in reasonable comfort. They took a small apartment near the city market district and lived off of the proceeds from the sail of Sarah's market.

Ireland was in a state of collapse at the turn of the 18th century. Economic ruin brought on by English restriction of Irish trade and repeated potato famines pushed Irish middle and lower classes towards Belfast's port and escape to the American colonies.

A single mother and child in these times had many challenges facing them. In order to survive, Sarah married Mr. Brickey the following year. Sarah's cash was depleted when she accepted Mr. Brickey's proposal. She was a good wife and he was kind to her daughter. Mr. Brickey only knew his wife as faithful and protective of her daughter. She was a loving wife and he was content with her in his life.

Sarah anticipated placing her daughter in a new life, away from the collapse of Irish culture. Ireland was a land of predictable outcome. Only the wealthy carried any thought of remaining while the fragile economy began to cause its natives to flee Ireland's shores.

Sarah intended to leave Mr. Brickey and return to her underworld and begin a new generation. That would happen only after she was assured that her daughter would be cared for. Until then she would continue to live with her earthly husband.

Chapter III

In the centuries of her immortal existence, Sarah had taken many mortals as her mates. She could have had any man that she desired. Her ability to look into a man's mind and adapt her appearance to fit the secret preferences that a man held in his mind was among her greatest gifts and provided her with the attention of the most powerful men of the region. She knew that everyman held his picture of perfection of a woman's beauty. Being able to change her form, she could become every man's ideal. No man could resist.

Her first mortal mate was a Norse warrior chief who came ashore in the early times of Dublin. The settlement became an outpost for Vikings who patrolled the shores of Ireland, Scotland and England.

Viking raiding parties first appeared in the area in the latter part of the 8th century. Their first attempts at collecting loot near Dublin led to a rout by the Irish of Ulaid and Umail. The following year they were defeated by the Irish King, Eo'ganancht Locha Lein. Viking raids in the years that followed finally overwhelmed Irish resistance, and in the year 836CE, Norsemen first wintered in Louth, near Dublin. Sarah had taken over the entrance to Dublin harbor shortly thereafter.

Her target was Olaf, the King of Vikings in the settlement of Dublin. Once she drew his attention, he was powerless to resist her. She lured him to her lair and held him captive with her beauty. His title within the community did not protect him from her assault, instead it made him the exclusive target of her desires.

Olaf later moved her into the village where she lived as his mistress. He had taken her hat and hidden it from her. After raising one daughter to the age of twelve, Sarah took the hat and left him.

Olaf was left with a beautiful child to rear. She came from a bloodline of Scandinavian heroes and leaders of her Father's culture. Olaf knew that the girl possessed the powers of her mother. He knew that she had the history of many generations of immortal life in her blood.

Her name was Esther. She was a beautiful child with the long blonde hair like the Scandinavians of her father's homeland. At the age of thirteen, she was already the most beautiful young maiden of Dublin. The Irishmen of Dublin saw few blondes.

Esther was a sight to behold. Her behavior in public was a spectacle and years ahead of her age. The Irish saw her as a melding of the two contentious cultures. They were often amazed by the child's behavior in public.

Norsemen had a long history of raiding the coast near the new village. There had been many territorial battles between Irish clans and Viking raiders. Irish locals were beginning to accept the foreigners in the village that the Irish called Dyflin or Duiblinn after the dark tidal pools of the River Poddle.

Esther's father tried to keep her under his control. She was two or three years younger than Nordic brides typically were before they married. Her beauty and sultry nature made those years quite difficult for her father. He spent as much time chasing hopeful suitors away as he did leading the people of Dublin.

Her dark eyes stood in contrast to her butter blonde hair and pale complexion. Village women gossiped over the beginnings of the precocious young woman. She had learned to use her supernatural skills early. It was apparent to all that she was not from their mortal world.

Even as a youngster, she captured men's attention and drew them dangerously near her as she flirted and toyed with their attention.

Esther's father could not draw attention to his plight for that would confirm the village's suspicion of the girl's origin. Olaf feared that village wives might harm her even though she was the daughter of the King. Esther. The King was not to be trifled with.

Esther continued to flirt with men twice her age and caused continuous disruptions in the village. Gossip said that she had already lured several young men into the barns and warehouses around Dublin and had her way with all of them. Her father was kept ignorant of this gossip. He continued to see her as an innocent child while men of the village sought to be among those who had rolled in the hay with the blond Princess.

The King intended that to have Esther marry a Nordic Prince of his choosing. He aimed to solidify the political connection between Dublin and the Scandinavian King in Norway. Olaf insisted that local men stay away. Little did he know that most found Olaf's continuing protection of his promiscuous daughter laughable.

The village told endless stories about Esther and her sexual escapades in the city public houses, away from the King who never frequented them. Olaf never knew that it was Esther who pushed the limits on her behavior. Those that responded to her lustful calling were the victims, not the aggressors.

At fourteen, Esther had matured into a flaxen haired beauty. She stood as tall as many of the Irish men of her village. They all knew that they were forbidden from showing an interest in her but gossip and bragging over young men falling to her ways of seduction made others willing to risk the King's punishment.

Learning about the problems her daughter caused in the village, Sarah secretly visited Esther to remind her of the plan to mate with a nobleman from Scandinavia. Sarah told her daughter not to risk of being impregnated by village peasants.

Esther was too passionate to mind her Mother's caution. Sarah's plan needed to be advanced because her daughter could not be restrained. Even at the penalty of death to anyone who tried to deflower the local Princess, men could not stay away. The list of men in Dublin who had sampled her passionate skills grew.

Another year passed. Esther finally turned fifteen. Olaf received a message from the King in Oslo. He proposed a marriage partner. He was to arrive in Dublin within days. The proposed groom was the son of a Danish nobleman. Esther became moody with the news of his anticipated arrival.

"Must I marry this stranger, father?" she asked. "I have plenty of men in Dublin who would like to bed me."

"You must marry a Prince, suitable to your station, Esther, and there is more involved than finding someone who wants to bed you," he answered.

When the young man finally arrived, Esther halted her local escapades. Prince Rolf was a tall lean and muscular warrior. His eyes were sky blue and his hair was the color of Fall wheat. Esther's mood changed. She took possession of the new arrival immediately. Following the lead from Sarah she used all of her skills to attract the new comer.

The wedding took place as planned. A house was erected for Rolf and Esther and they took their place among the nobles of Dublin. Local men continued to pursue her favor but they were spurned away. Dublin women held their collective breath that the Norseman would contain his bride's lust and keep her away from their husbands.

In the Spring, she delivered a daughter. This event brought a new wave of chaos to Dublin. Just as the village men gave a sigh of relief over avoiding being hung for giving in to the little tramp, the village was faced with the news that the child was raven haired and had eyes as black as night.

Months later, the scandal ended when Esther left her husband with her baby.

Despite his best efforts to avoid the controversy, Olaf could not bring his public to understand how his blond daughter and a Scandinavian Prince could have produced a dark haired, black eyed child. Before he could defeat the rumors that threatened his realm, Esther was gone. He no longer worried about her virginity, but he was left with the scandal over the child's origin.

Villagers learned that Esther could be seen, sitting on the rocks near the entrance of the Dublin harbor. The mystery of the child's beginnings was solved. They saw Esther raising her child in the manner of their legendary Mur'uchs. Those that saw Esther said that she sat upon the shore rocks singing Irish lullabies to her daughter. Both carried the physical characteristics of sea maidens. To Olaf's embarrassment, Esther frequently stood up as ships passed, waving joyfully to her old neighbors.

Esther's husband humbly returned to his homeland. The King knew exactly what had taken place but could not speak of it. Esther entered the world of the Irish Mur'uch and its pull on her was stronger than the Nordic Prince. Both Sarah and Esther got what they wanted from the King and the Prince. They got a female child with a strong mortal bloodline and the heritage of the Mur'uch.

Sarah's system of producing daughters with exceptional genes for beauty and politics had continued through the ages. She was determined to strengthen her realm with descendents of special blood lines of sea maidens and monarchs.

For several centuries, Sarah's daughters joined her in the domain of the sea. Each ruled their own region in Scandinavia, Ireland, Scotland or the Hebrides Islands of Shetland and Orkney.

Sarah's will to produce new generations had always been strong. She had been among the most prolific of her kind. In the role of Queen Sea Maiden, she encouraged her followers to produce their own daughters of good bloodline and increase their collective power.

Unlike the legends of other Mur'uchs, Sarah did not try to capture men and harm them. She wanted their bloodlines to combine with her own. There were no reasons to harm her prey or take them to the bottom of the sea as others have done. Since the first Norse warrior, she had lived as a wife to hundreds of mortal men of her selection. Sarah chose those who she saw best fit her needs.

To avoid producing a Merrow, she bedded her men frequently. This practice eliminated the chance of producing a male as male seeds were faster to the egg, but there were fewer of them and they did not have the sustaining power of female seeds. Sarah knew that female seeds surrounded the egg and prevented male seeds from approaching and ultimately fertilizing the egg. The male seed soon died, unable to get through to perform its task while the female penetrated the barrier.

Sarah learned to perfect this procedure and passed it on to her daughters.

Sarah believed that Merrows were worthless and they smelled and they lived a foul life among lesser Mur'uchs. They were good only to those who believed that they brought good luck. A few fishing villages kept

Merrows. They sat upon the rocks waiting on cases of wine and brandy to wash ashore or brought out by villagers. They were eunuchs, unable to attract a mortal female or even produce their own kind. They were to be eliminated from Sarah's world.

With her method, Merrows were avoided. Sarah drained her husbands daily. Once her mates lost their virility, she abandoned them in favor of younger ones. Sarah continued with her breeding with the youngest and strongest men that she could find.

She sat near the entrance to their village harbor and enticed the best of them with her beauty and ballads of Irish lore. When she had them wanting, she planted her hat where they could find it. Thinking that they were savvy enough to capture the hat and trick the beautiful mermaid, they would take her in and fall into the web of her design. She milked them of their seed until they could give no more.

The cycle went on until Sarah had worked the leading men of the coastal regions of Ireland and Scotland and produced daughters with the power to rule the mortal realm as well as the deep, dark lairs of the sea.

On the Scottish shore, off of the rocks near the mouth of the River Clyde, Sarah had been the wife of a village elder. He was the custodian of the castle of the King of Scotland. They lived in a small dwelling on the leeward side of a mound, sheltered from the westerly winds of the North Irish Sea. On the bench near the far wall from the drafty entrance, Sarah held her man in the powerful grip of her legs and arms and drained him for the third time today. The first was at dawn before his meal of wheat cakes and mead. The second was soon after she teased him back to arousal as he tried to escape through the door.

"I want every drop of your seed," she told him as she held him close to her after he had spent himself for the third time. "Give me another daughter," she said." She rose to place her soft belly near his face. He kissed the white flesh below her soft belly and grasped her round white rump in his hands.

"Give me more," she commanded! She slipped down over his chest and took him in. She groaned out loud. He tried to cover her mouth and contain her voice within their house. He removed his hand when she bit his fingers. Soon she let out another cry of triumph.

"The whole village will hear your howl. Contain your self," he scolded.

"They all know that we are passionate. Do they not?" she asked.

"Yes, they do," he said.

"We have two daughters already, Sarah. Why can we not have a son?" he objected. "With all of the time that we spend on this bench, a son should not be too much to hope for."

Looking down at her daughters sitting on a fur rug, she said, "Do you not enjoy the love and the pride that your daughters bring to your life?" she asked. They looked up at their mother and father and smiled before they returned to their play.

"I love them above all things. They have your beauty and may even have your passion some day, but a son is needed to carry on with our land and my trade," he said.

"We get what we get, old man," she chided.

"Old man!" he said. "Is this the way of an old man?" he asked. He removed the blanket and began to respond to her, once again. "The King will discharge me from my duties if he finds me in the arms of my woman every time he needs me," he offered meekly.

"The king knows the reason for your delay, husband" Sarah thought to her self. "He is as familiar with my knowing touch as you are, frail one," she silently mused.

He responded to her passionate demands beneath the covers. She stroked the back off his head when he was spent, once again. She them let him leave her bed and return to his daily chores.

"He needs more meat and less mead," she laughed after he left her shelter.

Sarah's mortal mates had always been village leaders, Scottish Kings, and Viking chieftains of Scandinavia as well as heads of familial clans of Ireland and Scotland. She was selective in her choice and had the beauty to capture and hold any man of her selection, even the King.

This King sent Sarah's husband away frequently so that he could lie with her. Sarah kept him drained as well.

"My wife complains of my lack of attention," he had said to her this morning. "She thinks that I am too lazy," he complained. The King was married to the beautiful Scandinavian Princess, Ingelbjorg of Finland.

She too was powerless to keep her King away from Sarah's seductive skills. She was insatiable.

"You are not lazy great King," she told him.

"But, the queen is more popular than I am. I need to keep in her good graces," he said. "I am the envy of all Scotland. To bed her, is the dream of all Scots and they would sooner rid themselves of me than to do without her."

Pulling back the covers of the bed, she asked," does she look like this?"

"I ache with passion," he said. He crawled into the shelter of her covers and took her into his arms. The rest was up to Sarah.

Sarah's voice was known throughout the world of Mur'uchs, Merrow and Selkies to be the strongest and most mesmerizing. Between trysts with her victims, she sat upon the rocks off shore and adapted her form into the woman of man's most secret dreams. The stronger his ideal mental image worked, the purer her form adhered to his wishes. She was simply, irresistible. No man could avoid her lure. She only took from those of powerful families. Only they could give her what she really wanted.

Sarah came from Scandinavia, among the coastal islands of Norway. Her mother was Estella, the Nordic Queen Maiden of the realm

Her mother was the sultry, raven haired beauty in a land of blondes. Norwegian, Danish and Swedish men held her image in their minds as they thought of the dark skinned and black haired women from Rome, and Spain that they lusted over while sailing in the Mediterranean. Their Spanish and Italian lovers were passionate. These Latin women not having to work as hard for their survival as Nordic wives, they found time to romance with the tall Scandinavian visitors.

Sarah's mother took the seed of Viking Chieftains who were lured to her rock after seeing her basking in the warmth of the summer sun. Sarah's older sisters held harbors in Denmark, Norway and Sweden.

When Sarah matured, her mother sent her on her way to find her own realm in Ireland and Scotland. No Queen wanted to compete with the beauty and allure of daughters of their own design. Sarah held the best traits of her mother and the mighty Norse Chieftain who was her Father.

In the days of the Roman occupation of Britannia she had lived with the General in charge of building the wall for Emperor Haden.

The Emperor had the wall erected to protect the more docile population of Britannia from the unruly and independent population of the northern highlands that he called, "Caledonia." The descendants of the first Celtic people who fled the Iberian Peninsula from pressure of the Mongols of the east took up lands in the highlands. They sought peace and independence but would never know either. The Romans called the natives of the highlands, "Pict," for the blue etched symbols on the skin of their bodies and faces. The Pict lived in a loosely related federation of tribes living independently in highland settlements.

The Pict harassed the Roman conscripted auxiliary who worked on the wall and the legions who were charged to protect them with their use of guerilla tactics. Being outnumbered by the thousands of Roman legions, they formed parties of twenty to thirty warriors and attacked the wall and the Roman tent encampment in the cover of darkness, killing hundreds of sleeping soldiers.

After her Roman General was relieved of his duties for failure to complete the wall and protect Britannia from raids on their villages and farms, Sarah lived among the Pict as a mate to Maelchon, a war lord of a Pictish settlement north of Hadrian's wall.

Maelchon and his young son, Breidi, attacked with a group of warriors who became known in the Roman camp as "the *guerriero espirito,*' ghost fighters. Covered in fire ash mixed with rendered animal fat they attacked the camp on the south side of the wall. Roman officers were unable to capture a Pict warrior to demonstrate that the enemy was not a ghost. The Pict beheaded and disemboweled the Roman guards and displayed their severed heads on their own pikes, driven into the rocky soil.

After years of trying to defend the wall, the Romans erected a second wall north of the first. It became known as Antonine's Wall. It was not completed before the Emperor recalled his army from Britannia, telling them that they would have to defend themselves from the unruly Pict. They returned to Rome to defend other parts of their empire. Sarah became a legend of the Pict.

Maelchon had been among the mortals who would help her produce the most beautiful and powerful sea maidens with dominate men.

Sarah's daughter by William, the Ballyhalbert fisherman, showed signs of being a beautiful siren herself. She was tall and slender and moved with a grace that belied her youth. She began to develop her womanly appearance early and Sarah encouraged her in perfecting her feminine pursuits.

In Ballyhalbert, Sarah's daughter was the talk of young men. She had learned to work her skills in subtly attracting their attention. She helped her mother in the fish market and made herself available to be seen by young men who passed nearby. She would have been the catch of Ballyhalbert if she would have stayed, but Sarah had plans that would take her away from this small village and the meager existence that held its people in poverty.

Belfast would not be the final home for Sarah's young charge. As soon as she matured, she would see to it that she secured a way out of Belfast and Ireland. Until then, she would patiently live the life of a merchant's wife. Sarah had all of the time in the world.

Sarah kept her daughter near her side while they worked the shop for Mr. Brickey. She did not want her seen by young men of Belfast who could barely make their own way in the trouble condition in the city.

This young one was destined to a special calling.

Chapter IV

Hugh Thomson began his life in Edinburgh, Scotland in 1660. His family originated in the Western Highlands of Scotland. Home was the small fishing village of Dumbarton. Then known as McTavish, Hugh's ancestors had existed in this region since the days of the high Kings of Dun ArdRigh. They were the custodians of the Stewart line of Scottish Kings back through a time before the days of Robert the Bruce, when Scotland and Ireland were part of the kingdom of Dalriada.

Thomson family roots began through the Lady DeSweyne, daughter of "Sweyne, The Red." She produced a son who she named Tamhais (known as Tavish or Thomas). His son became the first McTavish (Son of Thomas). As guardians of the castle at the base of Dun ArdRigh they were Jacobite supporters of the Stewart line of Scotland's Kings. In order to hide their Scottish loyalty, McTavish would change their surname to Thomson.

Hugh Thomson's ancestors learned to produce malt from fermented barley. Dumbarton sat at the mouth of the River Clyde in the Scottish highlands where the land was rugged. Their farm plots supported little other than barley.

Their malt was used as currency in the region, and the far reaches of the northern Hebrides Islands where they lived and traded peacefully with the Vikings of Scandinavia.

Vikings integrated with the people of the Scottish Highlands and the Hebrides Islands where native people benefited from the Viking ways of village law, fishing and ship building. The traditions of the Nordic people were introduced by Vikings who came to raid and decided to stay and improve their own existence.

The Scottish people of Dumbarton were known to be as rugged as their land. They lived in single room stone houses that were built on the leeward side of hills, near the shores of the North Irish Sea. These one room shelters helped protect the inhabitants from the fierce cold winds that crept through the walls like an invading army. Wood was not available in the highlands. Their stone houses had roofs supported with whale bone and they burned dried peat or brought their livestock in with them to help warm the interior.

Eight generations later, Hugh and his wife Margaret Craig Thomson abandoned the family barley malt trade, and crossed the narrow span of the North Irish Sea into County Antrim, Ireland. They settled in the city of Belfast and set up their business in a time when Belfast was at its worst. The streets were filled with destitute families who had been driven from their farms.

Hugh had worked the black smith trade since he was a young man and had taught his sons how to carry on with the business. The blessing of his trade was that it was somewhat insulated from the fate of Scot-Irish farmers who faced starvation from a string of potato crop blights and the ruination of Ireland in the Ulster Plantation Program and The Protestant Reformation.

Hugh began to plan for family evacuation when he heard about the land that was available south of Philadelphia. The economy around Belfast had been driven away, causing thousands to leave Ireland by boarding immigrant ships in the Port of Belfast.

"Someday soon, we will need to leave Ireland," Hugh said to Margaret as they sat in their modest kitchen. Like many Belfast tradesmen, they kept their living quarters at the back of the blacksmith shop where they lived comfortably with their sons.

"We have saved nearly enough but we need to keep it away from the landlord," Hugh went on.

"I checked at the port," William said, "and learned that we will need 20 pounds sterling for fare to Philadelphia for the four of us. We should look to book passage in a month or so. We should wait no longer," Hugh concluded.

"No dear, we shouldn't, but I am concerned about your health. You have worked too hard and I fear the soot air from the shop has only made your health worse," Margaret said.

"That skin flint landlord would raise our rent if he caught on to our new business dealings," Hugh said, gesturing with his blacksmith tongs. Margaret backed-up a couple steps to stay out of his reach. She had learned not to interfere in Hugh's frequent and passionate expression.

Thomsons were strong willed and passionate in all things. Hugh's metal working profession fit his personality perfectly. "Pound on it, until it fits," Margaret would say.

"I will check into a fare for next month, next time I deliver to the dock," Hugh went on, as he saw Mary step aside of his gloved gesture, and smiled at the gentle and compassionate way of his small but mighty wife.

Hugh left the following morning to learn what he could about fares to America, departure schedules and what they would need to take with them. At supper that evening, Hugh told his family about what he had been able to learn.

"The agent at the pier says that there are departures on the second of every month. Departure time is 0800 am. They begin boarding at 0600 am, so it would be best to arrive early," Hugh said. "I have purchased our passage for the second of next month, for the five of us," he concluded.

"Boys," Hugh said. "We need to finish these last few orders and collect our due as soon as possible. With that income we should be able to pay our way and give us enough to live on in Philadelphia. I understand that wagons are available that can be purchased for transport into the frontier lands," Hugh said.

Mary said," I understand that the conditions on those immigrant ships are deplorable. Those that have seen them say that they are filthy from hauling vagrants and felons from the jail."

"Yes, I know, but it is not a fault of their own, and I think that we are blessed for not being among them," Hugh said.

"I did learn some other matters about these ships, that the agent did not tell me," Hugh went on. "I purchased passage in a state room. It was twenty pounds more than steerage, but from what I am told and what I saw, this will be money well spent."

"Steerage conditions are very bad," Hugh continued, while Margaret listened to every word." Thank God that we do not have infants. Their mortality is the highest. One in five, I am told. Their systems will not tolerate the disease and filth on board," Hugh continued. "At least in the private rooms, there are two windows which we will be able to use."

"Our main concern will be food, water and disease on board," Hugh went on. "Diphtheria, cholera, whooping cough and measles have all been reported. Those in steerage have experienced them all, and we need to do all that we can to stay clear of them. As many as one in eight, among those in steerage, arrived expired or in critical condition, despite the fact that some ships had surgeons on board."

"I am also told that live animals are boarded and kept in pens near steerage for use during the passage.

"Well, enough of that for a while," Margaret broke in.

"I found out a lot," Hugh said, defensively, "and I am only trying to get us prepared for what is ahead," Hugh said.

"Yes dear, you are. It is just that this is so much to take in," Mary said.

"Well, anyway, word is coming back that Irish settlers have worked their way into the Virginia Territory, and a place called, The Shenandoah Valley," Hugh said. "That's the good news. I understand that good farm land is still available for the taking at the south end of the valley. Can you imagine boys?" Hugh said before he broke into a coughing spell and had to place his handkerchief over his mouth. "Can you imagine, we could even get back to grandfather's whisky making trade."

Hugh had left the malt and whisky making trade in Scotland when they came to Ulster. He had since mastered the art of working with iron, copper and brass in his shop. Brass hinges, straps and harness fittings were needed to supply the growing trade. Hugh could supply a good product at a lower price because of his sons who took no salary in the family business.

Hugh and Margaret Thomson lived a decent life amid a tragic period in Ulster Province. His blacksmith trade fed his wife and sons and gave them a solid roof over their heads.

Hugh and Mary knew of the Black Plague, that was causing panic around sea ports of England and Ireland. They had not discussed their concerns with the family, but the concern over all of these conditions in Ireland was too much to ignore.

While people starved, and begged on the street, the English continued to turn a cold shoulder toward the plight of Ireland. Their solution, despite outcries from colonial investors, was to put them on boats and send them to America. Orphanages, jails and poorhouses dumped their load on immigrant ships and out of England's sight before they closed. Someone else could clean up their mess and they did not have the stomach for funding their existence.

Hugh's plan for the family to travel together became as blighted as the Irish potato crop when he learned that his breathing problem was "Consumption." Both he and Margaret assumed that his coughing was due to the heavy, soot laden air of the shop. Now they knew that his lungs would never have the capacity to sustain his active life and would eventually take over his body, as the disease's name implied.

"Hugh," Margaret said, one evening "we need to make some decisions with this news on us. I would do almost do anything to be able to go to America as we had planned. But now I am fearful that the voyage would be your ruin," she continued.

Margaret knew that he would be unable to survive the two to three month passage and would have been sent back if colony leaders discovered his disease. It was a terrible realization to Hugh and Margaret. Their dream had been destroyed. All of the planning and dreaming of finding and settling their own land was for naught.

"It is up to you my dear," Hugh said. "I know that you are right. We have saved for this all of these years but I can not bear the thought of having my sons leave without us. We will never see them again."

Margaret said nothing, as there was not much that could be said to the drastic reality. Margaret had already decided that their sons, James and William, along with James' new wife, Mary Towes Thomson, would make the crossing alone.

Margaret and Hugh would remain behind and tend to Hugh's health as best they could. They would live out the fortune of their lives, as fate would have it. With some sense of pride, amid the devastating appointment, Hugh and Margaret knew that they had at least provided for a new start for their sons.

"Hugh, find strength in the fact that we have been able to provide our boys with the means to leave Ireland and start their lives anew. Without your hard work and sacrifice, that would not be possible. It is time for the Thomson Clan to leave Ireland and find room to grow and prosper and I know just the power to insure that happens, Mary said, quietly to her self.

"Excuse me dear, did you say something," Hugh asked.

"No, just thinking out loud," she said.

Margaret would have gone to the local parish and prayed about Hugh's health in previous times. With their Catholic traditions outlawed by the English Crown years ago, they had converted to the Presbyterian tradition. Now, even that was being taken away. Rather than convert to the Anglican Church, Margaret stayed home and talked to her God in her own way. She left organized religion for the earthly souls who sought to control its patrons.

The Anglican preacher probably had the doors locked anyway. The old Parish was always available for those who wanted to pray in God's house. "Anglicans make sure that you don't go in there unless they have the chance to pass the plate," Margaret mused.

Hugh and Margaret decided to hire a journeyman to replace William and James, so that they could continue to produce income and keep their English landlord off of their backs.

The streets of Belfast had once thrived with hundreds of shops and businesses. The linen district employed a good portion of Belfast's citizens. Flax from growers poured into Belfast factories to make fabrics in the manufacturing zone, by the port.

The Scotland and Ireland that they all knew and sang songs about were gone. The Irish tradition of melancholy song and verse came to be, once more. Ireland was now the land that they only saw in their dreams. It was a land which could no longer support them. Like a suitor who has found that the girl of his dreams has left him for another, they needed to leave the Ireland of their visions and move on to a new beginning.

Margaret frequently found families on the street with small children. She brought them in and made sure that they were warm and fed. She had her boys build a small shelter in the back. There were no beds, per se, but pallets placed on the floor would suffice.

As Margaret, brought in pots of mutton stew and soda bread this cold evening, the room came to life with the sounds and smell of a meal being enjoyed. "Here ya' go now love, take this and consider your blessings. We will worry about tomorrow, tomorrow and at least approach it with a belly full of warm stew," she said as she filled their bowls.

"This is awful, the way these people are being treated, Hugh," Margaret said after she left her guests in their room. "These people are being evicted from their homes as their husbands are being jailed for back payment of rent. What is our country coming to, Hugh?" she pleaded.

"The local Barrister posts these eviction notices by the hundreds," she went on. "They know what will happen. They know that people will have to leave their homes. I have even heard that judgments come down from the Barrister calling for people to be taken to the port and placed on ships to the colonies or Canada," Hugh said.

"I thought, originally, that religious persecution of Catholics and Presbyterians alike was the worst thing that the English could do, but it appears to me that most of these people have long forgotten about that, and are now faced with feeding themselves," Margaret said.

"Our country is turning sour, Hugh," Margaret said. "It has turned sour on its own people, and there are too few people who try to help each other," she said. "They put the Scots in Ulster as Presbyterians to chase the Catholics out. Now the English chase the Presbyterians out because they insist that they adopt The Church of England," she concluded.

"I don't know sweet woman," Hugh said as he held her close and placed his lips to the top of her head. "I don't know," he repeated.

"The two things that I do know are that our sons and our daughter-in-law will face a grueling trial aboard that ship. In the end, we have given them the fortitude to survive. They will raise their children in much better conditions than we have had," Hugh said.

"What's the other thing?" Margaret asked. "You said there were two." She went on in mock scolding of her beloved Hugh.

"Oh, yes. The second thing is that there is no woman in all of Ireland who has a bigger heart than you. You, single handedly, have fed and housed more destitute mothers, children and families than any other soul has ever done," he said.

"If you don't make it to the pearly gates and get in, then the rest of us sorry saps don't have a chance. That's the second one," he said. "I was just hoping that you would let me carry your baggage when you go. Maybe they won't notice that a heathen sneaked in," he laughed and kissed her on her forehead.

On the day before they were to depart, they had dinner together in Hugh and Margaret's quarters. There were feelings of sadness, anxiety and anticipation all mixed together. When they had eaten and the men went into the front room, Margaret reached into her cabinet and pulled out a bundle, wrapped in linen. It was obvious to Mary, whatever it was, Margaret was especially fond of it. Margaret stood holding the object with both hands, swaddled in fine, ancient linen.

"Dear Mary," she began, "I want you to have this and keep it always in your house with James."

"What is it mother?" Mary asked.

"It is many things to many people," Margaret answered.

"Here," she said as she placed the bundle in Mary's upturned hands. Margaret carefully removed the linen as Mary first laid eyes on what the old linen bore. It was an artifact of stone. It clearly was very old, for the surface of the marble stone had been rubbed smooth from generations of handling. Portions of its smooth, white head and legs shined where generations of women had clutched her in times of difficulty and peril.

"Women have clung to this icon for many years," Margaret said. "She has enormous power in protecting women and their families. She works in quiet and mysterious ways. She has the power to summon other Celtic deities of land and sea to bid her will. While we have been Christians for many years, we have always held on to our old pagan traditions as well. It can not hurt," she laughed.

"Take her and protect her, and never be afraid to ask her for her involvement in matters that are important to you, James or William. Do not be surprised by the ways that she chooses to appear before you. She oversees the work of all Celtic powers of legend and lore."

"She has been held by many women over the last few hundred years. The first might have been the Lady DeSween or the women of Johannes, Lochmatomy, Hay, Fordyce, or Craig. All of them married into the family since 1300. We are not sure where she joined the old McTavish clan or Thomson family, but she has stayed with us for many Thomson women."

"What is it? It appears to be in the form of a woman," Mary said, as she rubbed the surface of the grotesque little icon.

You shall pass it on to your daughter-in-law, some day. just as we all have. She will be there for many generations to come in America. It is time for her to leave Ireland with her people and join them in their new land and protect the blood line of Celtic woman."

"What is she called?" Mary asked as she looked down at the stone figure. It was clearly a woman Mary could see, for she displayed her female parts with lack of modesty. She was grotesque and yet she seemed comfortable in her open display of her child bearing role.

"She is *Sidhe Lena Gig*, my dear. You may call her Sheela na Gig, as some do. She is the ancient pagan goddess of women, wives and mothers. Her power protects Celtic women and their families and reminds them of their ancient roots to the Pictish people of the Scottish Highlands."

"Like I said, she is many things to many women, and that is why we have kept her to ourselves and not shown her to our husbands. She is all things that make a wife, a woman."

"Women of Ireland and the Scottish Highlands have been overseen by her influence for hundreds of years before the time of Christianity. We do not really know when she was first created, but we are sure that she has existed on country farms since the times of the Pictish people. Hugh's mother said that she believed that the McTavish clan that protected the Kings of Dun ArdRigh kept her among them. That is probably true, but she has been with the Thomson and McTavish clan for a lot longer than that. I suspect that she came to us hundreds of years before the time of the Romans in Scotland."

"She is beautiful, and yet, she is a bit crude. She is mysterious and she is also a bit strange. I see what you mean, mother. I will keep her always in our home. Thank you," Mary said.

"Yes, you do that sweet Mary," Margaret said as she held Mary close.

"She will always protect and look after your marriage, your man and your family. All that you must do is have faith in her powers and leave your concerns to her."

"It is time for her leave Ireland and follow Irish women and their families crossing the ocean to America. She is needed on those ships to protect the Irish who have risked everything in hopes of finding a better life in America," Margaret said.

"Please make sure that she looks after William as well. William is not married and probably will not be for years. He will need a woman with special power. She works in mysterious ways," Margaret said. "Maybe she will use her powers to find a woman for William. Heaven knows that she will need to be very special. Williams is a man of strong will. His wife must be as strong as he is.

"Yes, mother. *Sheela* will watch over William as well," Mary agreed.

She wrapped *Sheela* in the linen that had kept her secret for many generations. She unbuttoned her blouse and slipped *Sheela* into the deep cleavage between her plump breasts. "There you go Sheela," she said as she patted her bust. "You will be safe in there, where even Irish freckles don't go," Mary said with a grin.

That drew another embrace and a tear or two from Margaret. She would miss this stocky, affectionate woman that had brought so much love and happiness to her family. Mary wiggled when she giggled from the top of her head, over her plump bust and butt, all of the way down to her leprechaun like feet. Margaret would miss her and the generations of American Thomsons that come from this loving and caring woman.

"May God bless you and give you peace,…………and bunches of grandbabies," Margaret said before they left the kitchen and went in to join the men in the front room.

Chapter V

On June 02, 1721, James, Mary, and William took their bag of clothes aboard an immigrant ship bound for the port of Philadelphia, in the American colonies. The Belfast port was in chaos when they arrived. Hundreds of people were fighting to board the ship. Ugly scenes of desperation played out as hopeful passengers waited in line for weeks trying to get aboard any ship leaving Ireland.

A port official brought out a group of prisoners from a room in the back office. They clambered and fought to get aboard and away from their escorts whose duty it was to see them off. There were men, women and children in the group. They disappeared below deck.

Hugh and Margaret had paid for a cabin for James, William and Mary and themselves, as Hugh had said. Their room, intended for six passengers, was big enough for the three of them with room to spare. It was one floor down from the main deck and one floor up from steerage.

While standing on deck watching the port, William found a purple hat with seal skin trim at the foot of the railing. He thought maybe it belonged to Mary or another lady. He picked it up and placed it in the back pocket of his overcoat, intending to speak to Mary about it.

The impact of Hugh's decision to pay for the private room would not be apparent until they were out at sea and they saw the inhumane conditions suffered by those who could only afford steerage space below.

As they worked their way to their cabin, the stench from below decks was overwhelming. Mary placed a handkerchief over her mouth and nose as they descended the stairs. The smell of sweat and urine below their deck were strong.

They settled into their cabin as the ship was released from shore and made its way out to sea. James opened the window to allow fresh air into the cabin and to get relief from the odors below. Too exhausted to complain about the smell, they passed out on their bunks and slept fitfully through the night.

On the second day out, William took notice of a young woman who appeared to be traveling by herself. She was tall and stately. Her black hair cascaded gracefully down to the arch of her back. Her milky smooth skin stood out as if she had never spent time in the sun. By far, the most striking details of her appearance were her very large, pitch black eyes.

William knew that her eyes reminded him of something, but he could not recall what it was when he first met Temperance. "I will recall it later, perhaps," he thought.

Mary took to the young women immediately. Even though she wore clothes that brought attention to her slim shapely figure, Mary found her interesting to talk to. Temperance wore a corset that accentuated her small waist. Her dresses showed too much cleavage for Mary's taste.

"If I showed as much cleavage as Temperance, it would bring this entire ship to a halt," she laughed. "It is not my place to judge her and I can not imagine what I would do if I needed a man in my life," Mary said. "If you have it, flaunt it, I guess," she concluded. "I will just have to keep James busy with me so he doesn't notice her."

Mary liked Temperance none the less. She was soft spoken and a perfect companion for Mary. From the moment that William first introduced himself to her, he saw to it that the young lady spent no more time in steerage. He introduced her to James and Mary as "Temperance Brickey."

William had her join James, Mary and himself in their private room. There was space to be used in their room for another passenger. Mary was at ease with her since she had first met Temperance. That was fortunate since William, in his typical blunt manner, gave Mary no time to consider another choice. William and Mary made space for Temperance and the single bag that she carried with her.

"Is that all of your luggage dear?" Mary asked Temperance.

"Yes, I am afraid so. I did not have time to gather more," she said.

"Well, we will have to make due until we reach Philadelphia," Mary said.

Temperance said that she was the product of a French father and an Irish mother who had come from a coastal fishing village named Ballyhalbert on the Ard Peninsula.

"My mother and step father operated a small import and trading business in Belfast. It was once a lucrative, but it fell upon hard times like many others," she said.

"My mother came from a fishing family in a small village, Ballyhalbert. My father brought his catch in to his market on Shore Street where my mother sold his catch. She sometimes let me help," Temperance said. "Father failed to come home one afternoon after fishing, and mother never heard from him again. Over time we lost our ability to support ourselves and moved into Belfast. Mother met my stepfather there," Temperance explained.

"That is terrible, about your father," Mary said.

"It happens all too often in villages like Ballyhalbert. Captains often meet their death at sea. Fishing is a dangerous way of life. We sometimes say that if a Captain fails to return, that he has met and married a mermaid," Temperance said, smiling.

Temperance was very attractive, even seductive, Mary thought. "She might make a fitting wife for William." She had very good manners, and a presence about her that was at first, unnerving. She provided Mary with another woman to talk to and Mary was glad to have her. William would have to fend for himself.

Mary thought that some people are more noticeable when they enter a room. Temperance certainly had that trait, Mary told William. "It is her eyes, perhaps," Mary said. "They remind me of seal pup's eyes, dark and shiny," she said.

"That's it!" William declared.

"What's it?" Mary asked.

"Her eyes! Temperance's eyes are like those of a seal pup!" William declared.

"I knew that they reminded me of something in nature. I just could not place them," William said. "They are shiny black and moist, even as if they were tearing."

Mary remembered that Margaret had told her about the people of fishing villages along the northern shores of Ireland that she called, "Black Irish." They were said to have milky fair skin that contrasted sharply with their black hair. "Mother said that they were descendants of shipwrecked, Spanish Armada sailors who had found refuge and intermarried with Irish fishing families."

Temperance's raven black hair, and pitch black eyes made her quite striking in appearance and reminded Mary of Margaret's description of the Black Irish. Mary could not quite understand Temperance's quiet demeanor.

"She arrives on the ship with one bag and she is alone, yet she is as confident as if she had an army of suitors waiting to do her bid," Mary thought. "Strange," she said.

"Her one outfit was of high quality," Mary thought. "They were probably made in one of the old tailors' shops that once lined the street in Belfast's old manufacturing district. Commoners made their own clothes. These were certainly not home made. Well, it doesn't matter right now," Mary said to herself.

Sheela was still snuggled safely between Mary's breasts, close to her heart where she had placed it yesterday morning as they prepared to leave. She had not had a lot of time to consider the matter, but Margaret's talking about *Sheela's* powers made Mary feel safe. Even in these conditions.

"I am sure that you can care for one more lady, right, *Sheela* ?" she asked quietly.

As Hugh had predicted, the first sign of trouble came from the area where crewmen had placed live sheep, goats, pigs and chickens. Passengers began complaining of insect bites from bed bugs and fleas.

James found the ships surgeon on deck one evening as he stood at the rail, smoking a pipe.

"Sir," James said. "We need insect treatment in our state room, and I am sure even more in steerage. They must be coming from the animal stowage, below," James went on.

The surgeon acted as if he had not heard, at first. But, when James started to repeat himself, the man turned, looked at James and said, "Yes, we do need to address that. I will have crewmen spread lye and sulfur powder down, first thing tomorrow. That should take care of them."

As James was about to tell the surgeon about the stench coming from below, the man took a small flask from his breast pocket and took a swig from it. "Is there anything else, lad?" the surgeon asked.

"Yes, as a matter of fact there is," James began. The surgeon met James' persistence with a raised eyebrow and the look of impatience.

"Well, now that you ask," James said, his annoyance apparent. "The stench coming from steerage below is terrible."

"Well, that is a different matter son. That smell is common to all Irishmen, lad," he said condescendingly. "That smell comes from Irishmen who don't know what a privy is, or what it is used for. There is little I can do about that, short of telling your countrymen down there to use the privy, and to try emptying it every once in a while."

"What stinks is your attitude and the slop that is fed to these people," James said. He took a menacing step closer to the arrogant physician.

"What do you care lad? You are in a cozy state room, are you not?" the man asked.

William and Temperance were a few steps away, standing at the railing. It seemed to James that she spent a lot of time looking out to sea since they left port. She was with William as they were watching the sea birds follow the ship and looking out over the vast expanse of the ocean.

William was talking to Temperance, but James saw her turn around facing the surgeon, as if to listen to the angry conversation that he and the ship's doctor were having. William continued talking even though her witness to his words made him uneasy. "I must keep my words with the doctor civil, even though I want to throw the old drunk overboard," he thought.

"I care because these people cannot change their circumstances," James told the surgeon. "I care because they continue to be ill treated by the vermin brought aboard like those bedbugs, and the likes of you. You old foul smelling sot!"

"These people are sick," James went on. "They also suffer from being wet from sea water coming in from rough seas. There are no windows for ventilation and they sit in sea water and their own waste for days on end. It is no wonder that it stinks and if not addressed will only get worse," James said.

"There is no reason to resort to that kind of language, Sir," the physician objected. He glanced quickly at Temperance and then returned to James who showed clear signs of annoyance with the doctor.

"Those people live in these same conditions on the street. Here, at least there is a roof over their heads and they are fed, I remind you," the doctor said. He turned his head back towards Temperance. She was staring straight back at him. He cleared his throat with a loud, hrrrumppp, and a bit of a choke, before looking back at James.

James felt ill at ease with this conversation turning ugly while Temperance looked on. William had evidently not heard a word of James' quarrel with the surgeon. He was not as sure about Temperance who should have been far enough away to avoid hearing their words. She kept her eyes focused on the doctor, who began to sweat profusely.

The doctor suddenly turned his head towards Temperance and with a look of shock on his face.

"I will have to see after them," the doctor finally told William. "Please forgive my impertinence," he said to James. The doctor kept his eyes in Temperance's direction. "I will see to them immediately," he managed to say amid the choking and gasping sounds that he continued to make.

James looked over at William and Temperance. William was talking, facing the railing. She stood with her back to the railing with her arms crossed and a smile on her face. She then turned around and joined William.

Mary brought fruit and bread to supplement their own meals from the ship. As it turned out, Mary was much wiser than she might have thought. She found that the food served on board was rancid. The drinking water was foul and everything had mold on it after the first week at sea.

The smell from the animals, kept below, drifted in when they tried to eat the mutton and pork that they were given at the beginning of each day as their ration.

As they entered the end of their first week of the crossing, conditions on board began to take their toll on passengers' health. Mary saw people violently ill. They were probably sick from the filth, disease and vermin on board. With the ship surgeon as apathetic as he was towards his responsibilities, there was no where to turn to complain. James had not seen the doctor since he spoke to him several days ago.

James found that conditions in steerage were even worse than Hugh had prepared them for. They were stuffed into a single room, lined with bunks so narrow that only the smallest passengers could fit onto them. The stench grew with every day that passed.

"James," Mary said. "I can't stand the constant screaming coming from below. Those people are going to die. Can't we do anything?" she asked.

"Temperance dear," Mary said. "Have you seen anything like this?"

"No. It is deplorable," she said.

"I don't see how we can help, dear. The surgeon is an old drunk and seems to be helpless in offering anything to change the sure outcome of filth and disease. He promised to look after the problem but I don't see that he has," James said.

"Despite what your dear father said, I thought that there would be more facilities for passengers. This boat does not look like it was meant for passengers at all," Mary said.

"Well, it probably wasn't. Most of the ships come in from Canada, where they are loaded with wood and furs and taken to Europe. Ship owners have them stop in Belfast and Liverpool to load passengers for the return trip. It is almost like they were human ballast," James said.

Chapter VI

The ship surgeon stood along the rail late that evening. He smoked his pipe and took swigs from the flask that he kept in his breast pocket.

"Insolent twits," he said, recalling the conversation with the young Irishman. "They can not hold me responsible for the problems that Irishmen cause themselves," he mumbled on. "Who does that young man think that he is?" he mumbled.

Feeling the presence of a person approaching, he turned and saw the young, dark haired woman who he had noticed earlier. She wore a dark night gown that fell loosely off of her shoulders and down her shapely bosom and torso.

"What is it my dear?" he asked, as she stepped towards him. "You will catch cold in this night air."

She stepped closer to the physician. "You, Englishman," she called. "Just as that young man said, you are a contemptible, foul smelling old sot and your attitude towards your passengers is unfortunate. How can you treat these poor, unfortunately miserable people with contempt in their greatest time of need and vulnerability."

The doctor took a step back as she approached closer. "There is no need for that kind of language, young lady," he objected.

"Yes, forgive me dear doctor, "she said. "That was rather impertinent of me," she said. She moved next to him. She placed her arm around his waist. "You are such a handsome man, though," she said.

The doctor tried to free himself from her uncomfortable and

threatening grasp. He was unable to move away from her or relieve himself from her hold.

The young woman began to change in appearance before his eyes. Her black nightgown dropped onto the deck. She stood nude before his eyes, then her legs disappeared into a long tail. Still, she held him tightly. He tried to free himself, astonished by his predicament. He tried to scream for help, but he could not.

The top of her gown disappeared into her flesh. She held onto to him, bare breasted.

"Oh my God," he said. "What do you want from me?" he asked. "I am sorry for my behavior. I was having a bad day and did not mean what I said."

"You have had bad days, right, Madam?"

"Never," the creature answered.

"Please forgive me," he pleaded. "I have been on many of these voyages and seen many Irish crossing to the colonies. I have become too calloused," he explained."

"Yes, you have, Englishman," she agreed.

Her hands and lower arms were wrapped tightly around his waist. Scales began to develop on her tail and arms. They took a light green hue in the moonlight of the evening.

"Look at me. Do you not find me attractive?" she asked.

"Yes, of course, but........." he stuttered.

She tightened her grip around the alarmed old man.

He spit out his pipe as she squeezed the air from his lungs. The pipe clattered onto the deck. He made no attempt at picking it up. "Come with me physician," she said as she placed her other arm around him and leaned him into the railing. In a smooth movement, she lifted him from the deck and over the railing. He tried to scream, but she placed her webbed hand over his face. His scream came out as a muted mumble as they hit the water.

Temperance held onto him until his struggling ceased. They sank deeper and deeper before she released him to fall to the ocean floor, relegated to the other creatures of the depths.

Hours later, James asked Mary, "Have you seen William today?".

"No, I have not, not since early this morning. "He should not be hard to find. Find Temperance, and you will find William."

"I have been looking for the ship surgeon, and have not been able to find him," James said. "I even asked the captain if he had seen the doctor. No one seems to know where he is. Perhaps he is tending to the passengers in steerage as he should have been all along. I was going to implore him to do something for the people below before disease takes more of them."

"I don't know of any way to help them since there apparently is no law for caring for ship passengers. I am headed below to see if he is there," James said. As he turned to go down the stairs, he ran into William.

"James, have you seen Temperance this morning?" William asked.

"No. As a matter of fact, I was just asking Mary if she had seen her or the doctor. I am going to the steerage compartment and see if I can find the doctor there. He needs to tend to these people or there will not be any left by the time we arrive in Philadelphia."

"I will go with you," William said.

"I will go as well," Mary said.

As they came into the steerage compartment, they noticed the quiet chatter coming from the room. Something had changed. The moaning and groaning that had once filled the air, was gone.

"Perhaps he is down here after all," James said.

As they entered the room, they saw Temperance kneeling beside a woman and child on one of the cots. Temperance had a towel in her hand which she was using to wipe a child's face.

"Temperance," William said. "What are you doing here? You will pick up their sickness. Come away from there!"

Temperance looked towards them, and gave a brief smile before she turned her head and continued washing the child's face, head and hands with warm water and soap from a bucket beside her.

Mary looked around the room. She saw other passengers busily cleaning the walls and floors with hot, soap water. Two women followed Temperance's lead and wiped the brows of others who needed attention. Temperance continued with the young girl as her mother began to clean the area around the child's bed.

"Have you seen the doctor lately, Temperance?" James asked.

"Temperance turned and softly said, "No, not for a while."

"The Captain has not seen him," James said. "Where could he have disappeared on such a small ship?"

Temperance ignored James' question as if he were only voicing his own thoughts.

She went on to the next bed and began caring for another child. "Madam, she said to the child's mother, "would you please dispose of this water and bring a clean bucket? There should be more on the cook's stove," she said. "We will need to keep a supply of hot water for a few days. So, if you find the pot nearly empty, have one of the men refill it."

"Temperance, may I help you?" Mary asked.

"Surely," Temperance said. "Make sure that you wash your hands after each person, and keep your hands away from your own face. Here," Temperance motioned to Mary, "take one of these and place it over your mouth and nose."

Mary took the handkerchief from Temperance and tied it around her face. "I can not bear to see these innocent children suffer," Temperance said. "They suffer from the folly of a calloused old man. They deserve much better," she said peering into the eyes of the sweat soaked child on the cot before her.

Mary did as Temperance instructed without saying anything further. The atmosphere of the once filthy compartment had changed dramatically, Mary thought. Once there was constant moaning. The stench crept out of this compartment and entered other areas of the ship. Now, there was an air of peace in the room. People were taking care of the foul conditions on their own, with Temperance's help.

"We will need more hot water from the galley," Temperance said to William and James. "If you would, please dispose of the water from the drinking barrel and replace it with scalding hot water from the pot on the galley stove. The drinking cup and dipper need to be washed as well."

"We can use hot sea water for scrubbing, but we will need fresh water for bathing. Thank you," Temperance said.

Temperance then moved on to a group of women working at cleaning the floors and walls. Mary wondered how long Temperance had been helping these people. From the appearance of the women cleaning and caring for the sick, it must have been going on for several days.

"Would you please help me, ladies?" Temperance said. "We will need to dump the privy bucket and clean the area around it. If you will get one of the men to dump it overboard, we can use hot water to clean it, and the area around it. Thank you," she said.

"Of course," one of them said. "What ever we can do to help, we will be glad to do," the woman said.

Chapter VII

The Ship's Doctor was never seen again. The Captain had a search conducted into every space on the ship. He was not to be found.

"He may have fallen overboard," the Captain proposed one day. "That is the only possibility that I can think of, short of foul play. Strange," the Captain said. "I have never seen anything quite as perplexing. Usually, people make noise if they fall over board. No one seems to have heard a thing," he concluded. "We found his pipe beside the on deck," the Captain said. "That is all that is left of our doctor," he said to James.

"I am told that you and the surgeon quarreled recently," the Captain said. "One of the crew men said that you were angry with him. Should I be concerned with your behavior?" the Captain asked.

"If you are implying that I had anything to do with the doctor's disappearance, you are mistaken Sir!" James shot back.

"Well, you did have words with him and your anger towards him was witnessed as being near violent," the Captain claimed.

"The doctor has been on many crossings to the colonies. It is difficult to believe that he simply fell over board," the Captain went on. "He was an experienced seaman as well as a trained surgeon," the Captained claimed.

"Until I determine what happened to him, I must consider that there is a possibility that your anger resulted in his disappearance," the Captain said. "There is no reason to confine you to the ship's brig, since there is no way you could possibly escape, but consider yourself under custody until I can get this situation resolved," the Captain commanded.

Over the next couple of days the number of sick passengers began to decline dramatically. They were lively, once again. They came up on deck to breathe the clean sea air and get fresh drinking water from the barrel that passengers were now getting fresh drinking water from. The food did not improve much, Mary thought, but no one seemed to care that much.

Temperance had some way influenced the ship's cook to be more diligent in keeping his galley clean and free of vermin and rats.

She insisted that water be kept boiling at all times in the galley. She even caused him to clean the galley regularly. Not much could be done with dried meat and fish except to open their crates and barrels and get rid of contents that had turned rancid.

Temperance had the passengers tending to their own needs by the end of the second week. They assigned someone to dump and clean the privy buckets. They all began cleaning their own spaces, as well. Their outlook seemed to have changed almost immediately.

James, William, Temperance and Mary looked forward to their arrival in Philadelphia. Mary produced some relief from boredom by reading by the small lamp in the room. There no longer was a foul odor coming from below.

"Those poor people," Mary said. "How could they have lived like that?" she asked. "If it were not for Temperance, we would have lost many more. She did what that Doctor should have been doing all along. I wonder what happened to him?"

"How could the Captain hold you responsible for his disappearance?" Mary asked.

"I don't know, Mary."

"Is he to hold you when we arrive at port?"

"I don't think so, but he could if he does not find the cause of the doctor's disappearance.

James said, "We are truly blessed to have the means to avoid what our fellow countrymen failed to escape. Even on a ship hundreds of miles from Ireland they are still being treated like rubbish. Many of them have Temperance to thank for surviving this voyage."

"Yes, we are fortunate that father got into the blacksmith trade," William said. "That one decision has made the difference for all of us. At least we have some semblance of livable conditions while we escape the end that would come to us if we had stayed," William went on, as Temperance stood beside him. Her face was lifted into the brisk night air.

"This reminds me of the stories my mother used to tell me about their village on the coast," Temperance said. "Her people lived upon the sea as fishermen. She once claimed that her ancestors even came from the sea."

"I have heard of stories of sea maidens and mermaids," William interrupted.

"They are the Muru'ch," Temperance said. "The female is lovely and graceful. She has a fish's tail and scales up to her hips. Her upper body is said to be of a beautiful woman, milky white skin cover her breasts, shoulders and arms. She is said to sometimes wear a gown as white as sea foam, or as black as night, either trimmed in red and purple."

The Captain walked towards the Thomsons. He heard Temperance speaking of mermaids and the Mur'uch of Irish legend and his curiosity peaked.

He stood silent as he heard Temperance say, "The water in her hair glistens like dew in the morning sun. Her face and coal black eyes are sometimes capped with a hat. She is said to sometimes wear a dark sleeveless cloak clinging to her body, mesmerizing fishermen with the voluptuous curves of her body that show through the sheen of her velvety black gown."

"Does she sing to fishermen, like we have been told?" William asked. He listened closely to Temperance's intriguing story.

"Yes, she is said to tease men with the open display of her naked beauty. Her siren song is said to be irresistible as she sits among the shore rocks. But, if a fisherman comes near, she is said to slip into the sea, laughing at them as they stand mesmerized, trying to find her," Temperance continued.

As the Captain stood with the group he saw the beginning of changes in the young woman's form. He stood, listening to her tale, his eyes fixed upon her mouth as she spoke. He rubbed his eyes in disbelief of what was occurring.

The Captain could not believe what he was seeing. The young woman's lower body began to transform. It changed into a long sensuous form.

"How is this to be," he asked himself, still in shock of what was appearing before him. He rubbed his eyes again, and shook his head as if to shake this notion from his mind.

No one else seemed to notice that her lower body ended in a powerful fluke, like that of a porpoise. "Can no one else see this?" he wondered.

"Are you speaking of the sea lore of Merrows and Muru'chs?" the Captain asked, stumbling. His speech began to slur, his words unclear as he spoke.

"Yes. The men are called Merrows. They are said to sit upon rocks near the shore and look out onto the sea. They wait for cases of brandy to wash ashore," Temperance answered. Her coat, blouse and under clothing of her upper body began to disappear into her flesh. Her forearms turned to a light green, with the hint of scales working down to her wrists. Her upper arms were clear. He followed them with his eyes to where they met her soft, milky white shoulders.

Temperance continued to hold William's arm. She stood, partially behind him, acting as if she was shy over her sudden nakedness before the Captain.

The Captain was fixed upon Temperance as he listened to her voice speak of things that he had heard of since he was a child. He had never heard a person that knew so much of the tales of sea maidens and the sailors. His father had spoken of them many years before.

"There were old timers in northern fishing villages, like my father who told such tales," the Captain said. His eyes stayed focused on the half naked, she creature. Her raven black hair fell to her bare shoulders and down onto her naked breasts peered through.

"These are not simple sea lore," Temperance corrected. The Captain stepped back. The naked young woman's direct rebuke shocked him.

"In northern fishing villages, they are a fact of life," she sternly insisted, as she stood on her powerful, porpoise like fluke. She stepped out from her man, in the open sight of the Captain. He gazed at her soft, white belly and her breasts that appeared as she adjusted her air for his unobstructed view.

James thought that the Captain was surprised at the young woman's telling of ancient sea lore. "He had most likely never heard a women speak so frankly about a subject that village women avoided," James reasoned to himself. "Whatever it is he appears to be unnerved. Like the doctor was the other day," James remembered.

"Temperance was there as well," he thought.

William began to sense the direction and intensity of the Captain's fixed stare at Temperance. He looked at James to catch his attention, and then back on the Captain. William gestured towards the Captain, with a side nod of his head.

"Fisherman spoke of Muru'chs among themselves, but never spoke of them in the presence of women. All women of fishing villages feared losing their men to the vision of capturing a Muru'ch and taking her away, enslaved to her sensual beauty and insatiable sexual skills," Temperance boldly continued, to everyone's astonishment.

"It was said," the Captain stuttered, trying to regain his composure, "that Mur'uchs produced black haired children of light skin and haunting dark eyes. Some were born with slightly webbed toes and fingers. They were often found sitting upon the rocks near the shore looking out onto the sea as if waiting for someone to take them away."

"It is said that male Merrows bring good luck to all. He usually wears a red hat, cocked upon his head above his bulbous red nose. He is said to have scaly green skin on his naked body. His hair and teeth are said to be green and smell of rum and brandy," the Captain continued.

James and William watched the Captain. His face turned red.

"Can they not see this naked young woman?" the Captain wondered.

"It is no wonder that the female sea maidens seek mortal men from the land," William said, looking at the Captain becoming irritated at his stumbling foolishness, hoping to fill the awkward silence.

"Men get little joy from her because they can rarely approach as she perches on her rock near the shore. They lust over her. Her nakedness shimmers in the sun. Her wet breasts glisten. The light that of the sun reflects upon them, drawing seamen near," Temperance said unfailingly, pouring on the lurid detail of her story. She watched the Captain cling to every word of her description, returning to her place behind William.

"Peek!" she projected into the Captains mind. She cupped her breast, and exposed it from the cover of William's back. "Peek," she repeated into the Captains inner voice.

She stared deeply into the Captains vision. "Ah, he prefers blondes," she detected from his eyes.

Before the Captain's astonished glare, her hair changed from black to the color of wheat and then to snow white. Her eyes became sky blue and her skin, pale pink.

The Captain suddenly staggered backwards. He nearly lost his footing. He grabbed his throat, his eyes jutting from their sockets. His hands, still at his throat, were causing his own distress.

"He is choking himself!" William observed. "This guy has gone nuts," William said to himself.

"They seldom get near her before she slips into the sea. The sailor's lust for her touch is lost as she disappears into the waves, with the smooth movement of her hips," Temperance continued, pouring on her vivid and lustful imaging as the Captain nearly fell over, leaning towards her. His hands shook at his throat as they applied more pressure.

"It is said that she brings a storm or disaster if men pursue her. When a seaman or a sailor fails to return home, it is sometimes said that he married a mermaid," Temperance said, stepping back from the Captain as he stumbled towards her and fell at her feet.

"Captain, are you all right?" James asked.

Temperance's slowly began to return to her human form. The family did not see her transformation. They were completely unaware of the cause of the Captain's distress.

The Captain gasped, as he began to breathe normally. His eyes returned to their normal size. He finally stepped closer, removed his hat and bowed before Temperance.

"She had been playing him," James thought to himself. "What is she up to giving this risqué description to an old sea salt, like the Captain?" James, like the others were completely unaware of what had just occurred between the Captain and Temperance. They only saw the bizarre behavior of the Captain.

"Yes, sometimes experienced seamen disappear from their ship without a sign. Some believe that they have leaped into the sea to follow a maiden," Temperance said.

"So that is it!" James thought, nearly out loud. "She is playing the Captain and he is hooked!" James mused.

"On the sea, she is just as alluring as she is near shore. She sometimes cracks up boats and sinks ships as a delightful diversion. She laughs at the causalities that she brings upon sailors," Temperance continued.

"She can attract sailors from the decks of their ships. Those that can retrieve her hat and keep its secret, will cause her to forget her past and quietly give in to marry him. It is said that her sexual skills are far beyond mortal women. She can hold a mortal man as a slave to her lust," she said. The Captain was nearly incapable of taking more of Temperance's ploy.

"That is enough, Temperance," James said.

Temperance stopped. She stroked her fingers across the cleavage of her breasts and paused with a finger touching the soft valley that was clearly visible in her open neck dress. Trying to reclaim his composure, the Captain's face was still red. He recognized that this young woman was still drawing attention to her body.

"She uses her favors to keep her man from the sea," Temperance concluded. "Their sensual, alluring beauty and sexual skills are perfected in mature Mur'uchs. It is their very existence."

"Temperance! That is enough," James scolded.

Mary took a step back and placed her hand over her mouth in astonishment of Temperance's continued frankness. "Oh my land," she said aloud. James looked at Mary and held up a finger for Mary to hold her tongue.

Temperance stared through the Captain's eyes, into his mind. "You are a fool Englishman," Temperance spoke in the Captains mind. "Do you think that this gentleman actually did away with that old sot," Temperance projected. "He got what he deserved. Do we need to carry this further?" his mind's voice said.

The Captain wiped his sweaty brow, looked at James, and said "Please forgive my impertinence the other evening, Mr. Thomson. I had no right, nor reason to accuse you in the disappearance of the ship's surgeon. It is quite clear to me that he certainly fell overboard in a drunken stupor.

"Please accept my apology," he said as he tipped his hat and nervously stepped away. He looked as if he might stumble before he reached the stairs.

Temperance stood smiling at James, William and Mary.

"What brought that on?" William said. "You nearly caused the poor man to faint while he forgot to breathe during your lurid tale."

"He apparently did not want to pursue the matter with the good doctor further," Temperance said.

"He did look struck with Temperance and her tale, didn't he?" Mary said.

"Forgive me," Temperance said.

"No reason for forgiveness," James said. "It was quite apparent what you were up to. The Captain was hooked with your tale from the beginning," James said. "Thank you."

Temperance said nothing further. She took William's arm and turned to walk towards the rail.

The evening breeze and the stars above were a sight to see. Passengers came up on deck to feel the cool breeze of the refreshing night air.

Some days the seas were calm and little notice was given to the rock and roll motion as the ship moved along on its westerly course. Other nights, the seas kicked up with storms. The pitching motion of the boat as it climbed the front side of waves and then plunged down the back side was enough to cause seasickness among many passengers.

One night, the seas began to kick-up large waves onto the deck as Mary, William and James stood along the rail, watching the storm approach the ship. Temperance was below helping a young woman giving birth.

The waves began to severely rock the ship as the ship plunged through the storm. Crewmen were unable to perform their duties aloft on the masts. They came down and busily began lashing cargo and supplies to the deck.

Mary could hear the timbers of the masts creaking and popping with the force of the storm. It drove waves crashing into the ship and over the deck.

"*Sheela*, help us through this time and keep us safe, sweet lady of

Ireland. I do not know your powers, but I ask for you strength wherever you find a way to lend yourself."

She could feel the warmth of the stone against her skin, as she held onto the icon between her breasts. The outside air turned cold as waves tumbled over the ship, its bow diving into one wave after another. A huge wave came over the top and caught James and Mary in one swift motion.

They took a position against the bulkhead and held on. Mary grabbed the handrail behind the water barrel, as the wave pushed her from her sitting position. she caught herself, she lost sight of James when she regained her balance.

In panic, she clutched *Sheela* in her hand and against her bosom with both hands. "No," she screamed as James was swept overboard with a wave that crashed Mary onto the deck.

"James?" she cried." She held her clutch to *Sheela*, not knowing what else she could do as the waves pounded the ship and tossed it in one direction and another. James was gone. She could not rise to her feet as another wave pounded her against the bulkhead. She clung to the icon with all of her might.

When Mary finally rose, she saw James on deck where she saw him fall overboard. Temperance's arms were wrapped around his waste, holding him erect. James was limp and his clothing was soaked. Temperance turned James and herself with her back to Mary and covered his mouth with her own. She blew three quick breathes into him.

James sputtered. He hacked up sea water and began to breathe on his own. Temperance squeezed James firmly. He hacked up more water and began to cough. Moments later he stood on his own and Temperance released him.

"Where did you come from?" Mary asked.

"I was nearby," Temperance answered.

Mary ran to James to help him get to his feet. Just as she reached James, another wave came over the railing and slammed her against the bulkhead once more. Temperance moved James towards Mary and moved them around the corner to the bulk head.

Temperance led James and Mary to safety of their room below.

Mary leaned back on her bedding. She said nothing but she wondered how Temperance was able to get to James. She was sure that she saw him swept overboard.

"How did she have the strength to rescue me from being swept over the rail, into the sea and certain death?" she wondered. Mary relaxed and clasped *Sheela* against her chest and closed her eyes. "Thank you," she said quietly.

Finally, they approached the port of Philadelphia. The excitement of the crew and passengers lifted everyone's spirit and filled everyone with anticipation. The Captain came to the deck and called for the crew to make ready for arrival at the port. When he saw James, William, Mary and Temperance he stepped back, out of sight.

Crewmen scaled the rope ladders to the tall masts and rigged sails, and began to release them for storage around their long wooden arms. As they approached the dock, crewmen threw dock ropes to workers below that secured them to the pier.

The sight of the confusion and the havoc on the landing was more than passengers could take in. Unsuspecting arrivals, delirious at having survived the passage rushed down the gangway to the dock where they were swiftly taken away by hordes of boarding house agents working for landlords of Philadelphia's Shanty Town.

More steerage passengers swelled out from the bottom floor and onto the dock as James, William and Mary looked on, overtaken by the calamity of the sight before them.

Passengers wobbled down the ramp on legs that had not stood on land for two months. They were met by others who showed them towards one direction or another, and to waiting wagons where others were being shown aboard.

Chapter VIII

When most of the crowd had cleared the pier, James, William, Temperance and Mary gathered their few belongings and left the ship. James saw the Captain standing along the railing when the passengers left the ship. James looked towards him for a moment and saw that the Captain was watching the four of them. Neither gestured to the other. James and his party disappeared down the ramp and into a sea of beggars and confused passengers.

Several women saw Temperance leaving the ship and came to her to offer thanks for her aid.

"Thank you," they said. "Thank you for seeing to us."

Beggars pulled on Mary's arm while street thugs pulled on William and James. They tried to pull them into a waiting wagon.

Others were shouting, "This way for housing." Some said," This way to boarding houses."

The scene was overwhelming. James pulled Mary, Temperance and William through the crowd and away from the havoc being played out before them.

"Come this way," he said. "We can walk this away and get away from all of this mess so we can see what we should do."

Mary, Temperance, James and William finally located an inn for the night. They would begin their search for services in the morning. The sea port and the streets nearby were swimming with thugs trying to get passengers' last few coins.

Thankfully, Mary, James and William were able to pay for their first night stay. William and James took one room, while the ladies took another, down the hall.

The ladies entered the room, which was plain in appearance. There was a wash bowl and pitcher on a stand, along with a couple oil lamps that lit the room.

While Mary was changing into her night gown, she took *Sheela* from her undergarment and placed her on the dresser. Mary saw Temperance look towards her when she took the linen covered object from the security of its hiding place and laid it on the dresser. Mary knew that Temperance was curious, but she did not immediately say anything.

Mary was still a bit struck by Temperance's recall of the old Irish tale about the sea maidens. Mary had not heard that story before and was taken aback by Temperance's recall of the tales details and her frank language used in front of men.

Uneasy with the silence, Mary picked up the icon and took the linen from it and showed it to Temperance. "This is Sheela, Mary said.

"*Sidhe Lena Gig*", Temperance corrected. "She is the ancient mother of Celtic women and the protector of woman kind. She is the maiden mother of all things Celtic."

"Yes," Mary said. "James' and William's mother gave her to me before we left. She said that it had been in their family for many generations. She comes from the times in the Scottish Highlands, where the Thomsons came from.

Are you familiar with her?" Mary asked.

"Yes," Temperance said. "She has been among Celtic women of the Pictish people for centuries. She works in mysterious ways among her people and those who place their fate with her."

William and James were down the hall preparing to rest from their long day. "Temperance has been a great benefit to Mary and William," James said. "She has been a friend to Mary, who might have been a bit lonely without her. She certainly showed her strengths in pulling Mary and I back from the sea. She also freed me from the Captain's suspect in the disappearance of the doctor. We are truly grateful to her."

"What are her plans, now that we are in Philadelphia?" James asked.

"Her plans?" William asked.

"Yes. Is she going to stay with us, or does she have family to find here in the colonies?" James asked.

"We have not talked about her future, and I suppose that you are right. We need to have a talk. For me, I would like to have her stay with us as long as possible," William said. "She seems to bring good fortune for us. Although I do not know much about her past, I am certainly attracted to her," William said.

"She is very attractive," James said, "But what of her knowledge of the sea maidens and her frank recall of their story. Does that not concern you of a prospective wife?"

"She must have connection to fishing villages of the north. Tales like those of Merrows and Selkies are told by old timers among them," William answered. "Sailors and fisherman from Ballyhalbert and other villages live among these tales. In the old pagan times they needed such tales to understand their remote and stark existence. Obviously, she heard them spoken by her family as a child."

"I have heard of them as well," but I have not heard their telling in such lurid detail," James said.

"It impressed the Captain," William said. "He was taken with Temperance and her detailed description of mermaids and sailors. For some reason, he no longer needed to resolve his questions about the disappearance of that old drunk doctor after he heard Temperance's tale.

"Perhaps something she said convinced him that there was an explanation for the doctor's disappearance that did not involve you and your anger with him," William said.

"I suppose so," James said.

The sign over the door at the inn, had read, "Cash in Advance. NO IRISH," as they entered.

James, William, Mary and Temperance had the good fortune to collapse in their beds that first night, without having to face further reality of how Philadelphia greeted its new Irish arrivals.

Next morning, they set out to find supplies and a wagon for their journey. They had no real plans or intended travel direction for seeking farm land. They only knew that they would need horses, a wagon and tools before they could set out on the search that would get land for them.

Their first stop was a wagonwright shop on the edge of town. Not knowing whether they would be able to get what they needed and leave immediately, or whether it would take more than that, they entered the shop to find someone who could tell them what they needed to do.

"James, here is a wagon maker's shop, let's see what this is all about," William said. As they entered the shop, they saw workers stacking strips of wood, sorted by size. They were unloading a wagon of wood slats and taking them into the work shop which was neatly organized.

It was a small facility for the amount of work going on there. There were groups of workmen working on wagon frames in different stages of completion. Craftsmen using draw knives carved the frame work of the wagon body, while others worked on sides and ends of the wagon box. All were busy with the three wagons being worked when James and William walked into the shop.

"May we speak to the shop owner? "William asked a worker at a bench. The man turned his head to the left, as he continued his work on a drawing. James and William walked over to the man who appeared to be working with building plans, and asked," Are you the owner of the shop?"

"Bitte?" The man said in an unrecognizable language, as a second man approached.

"Excuse me, gentlemen. This is Herr Kriegler," He said. "His English is not very good. How may we help you?" the man asked. He seemed distracted by the appearance of Mary and Temperance who stood outside of the shop entrance.

"We are interested in purchasing a wagon for our trip south." James said. "Can you tell us what we need to do to purchase one?"

"Will you be paying cash for your purchase?" the man asked.

"Yes, I suppose we will," James said.

"Well," he hesitated, "these wagons take our workers eight weeks or more to build, depending on the size you have in mind.......We have good availability of parts from the lumber mill and the black smith and wheelwright at this time, so that should help the waiting time," the man rambled on.

"We have made these Conestoga wagons in two or three different sizes."

"What did you call them?" William asked.

"They are Conestoga wagons. The name came from a river valley near German Town, up north where Mr. Kreigler is from in the Conestoga Valley. They are built for rugged use on the trail between here and the southern territories. They also make sturdy farm wagons for those that settle along the trail and begin to work the land." he said. "Any other type of carriage or wagon would be torn apart on the rough road down to Virginia and North Carolina. These are made just for that trip," Mr. Hockensmith said.

"And the price?" James asked.

"The bigger ones, used for freight, cost 200 pounds. The smaller ones are about 150 pounds."

"Do you have one finished?" James asked.

"No," the man said. "We don't, and it will take a couple of months to build one for you, unless you need a freight wagon. I do have one of those," he said.

"I am sorry, you seem to have the money needed, but I will have to have half of the price as you order it," he said.

"No, the twenty foot wagon should be enough" James said. "We only have the four of us" James continued. "Here is your seventy five pounds." James said as he reached into his coat pocket and produced a pouch, pulling out the required amount.

James was told that they could return in a month to see if workers had it ready. "What name on it please?" Hockensmith asked.

"I am sorry. What was your name?" the man asked.

"James Thomson," he answered.

"Sorry, we have problems with Irish folks these days." The man explained, "I do feel for them, but they cannot pay their way, and many of them are too sick from the crossing, to even work enough to pay for one. Philadelphia has not welcomed them as they expected, I am afraid."

"Yes, we have seen that," James said. "They escaped poverty and starvation in Ireland, chanced losing their lives aboard those ships, and finally arrive here with more need than they had when they left," James said quietly.

Temperance and Mary remained out side of the shop. Something had caught their attention and they were discussing it. James and William did not see the ladies, but Herr Kriegler watched them.

Not willing to continue on that issue, the man said, "There are other carriages and wagons being built in Philadelphia," he repeated. "These are the only ones that will survive the conditions on the wagon road. Road ruts and river crossings would tear a common carriage apart. Conestoga wagons are sturdy and made to handle these conditions, but they take some time to build. It is fortunate that you came here first. There are cheaper wagon choices that could be made, but if you plan to take the wagon road to the Carolina Territories, you need something that will get you there on the rough portions of the trail."

James tipped his hat and they turned to leave the shop, "We will begin work on your wagon as soon as I get workers to begin."

"Since we have to wait, and need something to do for a couple of months, how about hiring William and I to do whatever work you need done. We are not carpenters or wheelwrights, but perhaps we could bring in parts and we are journeymen metal smiths and metal fabricators. We worked in our father's blacksmith shop and produced a lot of the same parts that you appear to be using here," William said.

"Hmm," he said, pulling on his long beard, as if would help him find an answer.

"James and I are good workers," William said eagerly. "We are experienced at making iron hinges and straps," James continued.

Hockensmith walked out to the front of the shop and removed a sign that had held Temperance's and Mary's attention for the last few minutes. It read, "HELP WANTED, NO IRISH NEED APPLY."

"Excuse me ladies," he said nervously. "We do not need this."

"Sorry, again for not treating you with the respect that you probably deserve," Hockensmith said. "We seldom see Irishmen coming off of these boats with skills. Usually they end up in Shanty town on the outskirts of the city," he went on.

"The Irish have gained themselves a poor reputation in Philadelphia and on down the wagon road," Hockensmith said. "Many have taken land along the trail and are not willing to pay for it. Penn has instructed his agents in this region not to try to sell land to the Scotch-Irish. They sit on land as squatters, having no intention of paying for it," Hockensmith explained.

James looked at William, and saw that his brother was not taking this news any better than he was. The bad news did not sit well.

"If you are willing to work at bringing in deliveries and helping with the metal work, I will ask Mr. Kreigler to put 20 pounds of your down payment towards your team," he went on.

"That seems fair," James said. "What was your name sir?" James asked.

"The name is Hockensmith. I work for Mr. Kreigler. He came down from Germantown at the request of Mr. Penn to set up a shop to build wagons. They use them up north in the Conestoga Valley. Herr Kriegler is as much responsible for designing these wagons for the frontier as anyone. It is his design and he continues to improve it as he learns how his wagons fair on the trail."

"He recently began to adapt his design to handle the rough road by building them so that the center of the wagons, mid-way between the front axle and the rear one, contents would be less likely to roll around. He also makes the rear wheels bigger than the front, and even bigger than wagons made in London. That allows the wagon to pass over ruts and holes in the trail with much more ease. The bigger the wheel, the bigger the hole it can pass over without becoming stuck. Pretty ingenious, I think," Hockensmith concluded.

"Anyway, just a moment," Hockensmith said, as he approached Mr. Kreigler at the desk. Kreigler turned in his chair and leered at the Thomson brothers. When Hockensmith returned, he said, "Mr. Kriegler is not real happy with this arrangement, but I told him that you were blacksmiths, so he left your contract up to me," Hockensmith said.

"I will see you both at 0700, and don't make me sorry for giving you this opportunity," Hockensmith said.

"Thank you sir, you will not be sorry," James answered. "Can you direct us to a boarding house or an inn nearby, where we may take a couple rooms," James asked.

"Try the boarding house down the street," pointing to the big white building. "Their rooms are reasonable and clean. If I were you, I would act like Englishmen, and I would also distance myself from Shantytown. Any association with that place will do you no good," he concluded.

"What is Shanty Town?" William asked.

"It's where the Irish find themselves when they cannot locate employment and don't have enough money to leave town. It is a seven hundred mile walk down the trail to the Carolina Territory. That is a long walk," Hockensmith said. "Settlement bosses try to keep them all out of there. No one will hire them. They have fought, looted and rioted themselves into a corner, and now they suffer from their own doing. There are a few lace curtain Irishmen in Shanty town who try to make a go of it, but they are held back by the reputation of their kinsmen."

"That's about the way we are treated in Ireland," William said.

"If you tell the inn keeper, down there, pointing towards the boarding house, that you are Irish, he may not admit you. You might as well learn how to avoid being caught up in the problems that your countrymen have caused here," Schmidt said.

William was insulted by the remark, and started to remind Herr Hockensmith who had caused who's problem, but James grabbed him by the sleeve and pulled him out of the shop.

"Did you not hear what that man said James? William asked.

"Yes, I did. But in view of everything that apparently goes on around here, he is probably right. For the time being, we need to avoid being known as Irish," James said. "All we want to do is survive here long enough to get our wagon and get out of town. Let's put our Irish away long enough to get that done. Then if you want to pick a fight with everyone who does not like Irishmen, that's your business. Don't forget, we are really Scots. Right?" James asked.

"No. If we lived in Ireland, we are Irish," William belted out!

They left the wagon shop and walked down the boardwalk to the "Philadelphia Boarding House," as the sign said. Below that sign was another. "NO IRISH," it read.

"Ahhh, for the love of the Saints!" William started. James turned around and pointed his finger at William in warning.

William, Temperance, James and Mary went in any way, William was still huffing and puffing over another insult to the Irish. They approached the clerk and said, "We would like two rooms for two months please," James said. The clerk looked up and pointed to another sign that read the same as the one at the door. "NO IRISH."

"Ya' can take your bleedin' sign and shove it up your bleedin' arse," William belted out.

"Just a minute sir," James said, as he turned around and gave the scolding look that William was familiar with from his older brother.

"Put your pride away," James scolded.

"We're English. Tell us the total and we will pay it now, kind sir," James said to the clerk.

"Eight pounds, fifty, for two months," the clerk said

James took out nine, one pound coins and placed them on the counter. "This is our two month's rent," James said. "For two rooms and a bath, that seems a lot to me."

"That is kin to robbery mister," William broke in.

"The bath is not included in six pounds fifty," he said, "I'll take this extra fifty to satisfy that," he continued. "We allow no drinking and carousing in our rooms."

"What drinking and carousing do you have in mind there, Buster?" William asked in anger. "With the way you people treat your guests, it is no wonder they drink," William reasoned.

Without another word, the clerk took the coins and handed James two keys. They read "4" and "6."

They turned and took Mary and Temperance up to their room. The rooms were basic, but seemed to be clean. There was a wash stand, and clean beds with two sitting chairs next to a reading lamp. There were curtains on the windows that were open, letting the breeze in from the port. It looked over the view of busy streets below. The bath was down the hall in a room. There was a sign hung on the door that read, "Vacant," on one side and, "Occupied," on the other.

"How, fancy,"…….William said. "Vacant and Occupied is it? Well then, I'll have the vacant."

They had lived in much worse conditions on the ship. "This will do fine," James said as he handed Mary the key for number 6, next door.

"This will do fine for now," Mary said as she placed her bag on one of the beds. "This will do just fine," she said. "This is all right, right Temperance?" Mary asked.

"Yes, this is fine. Thank you," Temperance said.

James ordered water for Mary and Temperance's baths. "We could all use one. No wonder they don't like Irishmen. We must stink like a load of two week herring."

"We'll be back shortly. Enjoy your bath," James said.

James and William walked out onto the street. The activity around the port from yesterday's landing had subsided. Irish beggars still lined the streets, standing at corners and along the covered boardwalk. Traffic on the street and walks were stifled with Irish families taking shelter under the boardwalk covers with their few possessions, packed up behind their backs. They sat leaning against the walls of stores and shops looking out in the mass of people. Their eyes and expressions carried blank stares. Each held out their hand as James and William passed.

"I had the most strange and vivid dream last night James," William said. "It must have had something to do with our talk about Temperance before we went to sleep. You know,….the mermaids and all of that."

"Yes, what about your dream?" James asked.

"Well, it was so vivid and real," William repeated. "I was in a strange place, near a fishing village, perhaps. I am not sure. There, sitting upon rocks, near the shore, sat Temperance. She had a long graceful tail like a sea lion or fish, and she was naked above her hips."

"Whoa! That was a quite a dream brother," James interjected.

"Yes. Well anyway, she sat there looking out to me as I came ashore, wet from swimming as if I had been in a ship wreck. Her singing brought me to shore. I suddenly stood up among the gentle wave wash and saw her sitting there. Her long back arched as she brushed her black hair that flowed from her head to her hips with a sea shell comb," William finished.

"Is that it?" James asked. "You are going to stop there?"

"Well, there was more, of course, but I am not going to tell you about it," William responded.

"No" William said as they crossed the road among the traffic coming and going on the street. At every corner, Irish sat on wooden crates with their hats turned up, waiting on a little mercy. There were begging men, women and children everywhere.

Nearly every shop had a "No Irish," or "Cash Only," sign posted out front.

The only people who approached the beggars were from the work farms and mines. They continued to look for cheap labor among the new arriving immigrants. "I was told that they offer shelter and food for a three year contract of servitude. That is pretty pathetic James," William said.

"They might be better to take the offer than linger on here," James said. "If no one wants to hire them here in town, they are doomed if they stay in town. That may be the only way that they will ever get out of here. They spent every bit that they had to get here, and now they don't have enough to move on. The problem seems to be that they come off of those ships in such numbers that it takes weeks and weeks for them to figure out what they should do. Thousands arrive behind them, keeping the numbers higher than Philadelphia can work them in. The other problem is that they don't know any better and no one will speak to them about avoiding problems or showing them the way."

James and William went on to the dry goods store a few buildings down the street to purchase pants, shirts, boots and socks for themselves. They stood in front of the mirror and looked at their new outfits.

Then they began to look for a few dresses for Mary and Temperance. To their surprise, the dresses were already made and were stored in boxes on the shelf. They were used to having their clothes hand made by a family member or a tailor.

"What size are they, the clerk asked?

"I don't know what size they are, Madam," James answered clumsily. "They are about your size, miss," James answered. He looked over at William. James had a, "don't do it," look on his face.

"William looked the clerk over, and said, "Well, may be a tad bit smaller."

The woman's face turn beet red. William watched as she hastily spun around, lifted her trailing dress above her boots and marched away. William followed her, mocking her walk and swing of his hips. She walked away with William immediately behind her.

James tried to grab William by the arm, but it was too late. William lifted his pant cuffs by the sides of his pockets and swung his backside as he followed the clerk.

"Stop it William," James said quietly. It was too late. The clerk turned to point to the dresses, when she ran back into William still following her with his pants lifted over his new boots, swinging his behind.

"Well, here you go then," the red faced clerk said. "Will that be all?" she asked.

"No. Not quite. We will be taking these two pairs of britches and four shirts each," James said. "We will need suspenders, hats, and boots, as well."

"Irish, are ya'?" she said, as James listed the last few items. The clerk looked at the sign behind the counter. It read,"No Irish."

"We're English Madam, thank you the same," William claimed.

"Sure ya' are, and I am the Princess of the Nile," she said.

"Glad to meet you Princess," William mocked.

James took out five, one pound coins and placed them on the counter. The clerk looked relieved and swept the coins toward her.

"The Missus and lady will be needing hats and boots as well," James added.

"Will that be all then....... gentlemen?" she asked.

"Yes," James answered. "For now, that will be all."

As James and William began to leave, William turned and asked the clerk,"Irish are ya' now?"

"No. Certainly not. My husband and I came from London," she said.

"Imagine that," William said. "She's English ya' know. About as English as a Sheppard's pie, I suspect," he quipped.

James took William by the arm and helped him out through the door. "Are you having fun William?" James asked.

"Yes, as a matter of fact, that was fun," William answered. "It is either laugh or rip their bleeding heads off. Which do you prefer, big brother?" William asked.

James laughed and walked William away from the store.

"The prices for clothing and shelter are really high. Don't you think so James?" William asked.

"They surely are," James said. "The faster we can get our business done and move out of here, the better."

Chapter IX

When James and William returned to the boarding house, Mary and Temperance took their new clothes and left the bath for James and William who gladly took their turns in the steaming, soapy water.

As Mary and Temperance rested in their room following their baths, they heard singing coming from down the hall. It seemed to be coming from the bath.

Of all the trades in England, a beggin' is the best
For when a beggar's tired, you can lay him down to rest.
A beggin' I will go, a beggin' I will go.

I got a pocket for me oatmeal, and another for me rye
I got bottle by me side to drink when I am dry.
And a beggin' I will go, a beggin' I will go.

I sleep beneath an open tree, and there I pay no rent.
Providence provides for me, and there I am content.
A beggin'…….

"William!" James said as he pounded on the bath door………….
"Stop it!"

When William finished his bath, the four ventured down the short staircase and went into the dining room. They had not eaten since yesterday.

As James began to sit, he saw a pair of children, peering through the café window from the boardwalk out front. The boy had on a pair of overalls and shirt, with an eight sided newsboy's cap on this head just as he had worn as a lad. The girl was a bit smaller. She wore a bow in her matted and tangled hair. She had on a tattered dress and an infectious smile.

As the waiter came over, James said, "Please get these children something to eat.

"We don't feed the Irish here," he said.

"Well, ya' do now," William said. He slammed a one pound coin down on the wooden table with an open palm. The noise caused the ladies to nearly jump out of their seats. Those around them turned to see what had happened.

The waiter hesitated taking James' order for the children. Mary noticed Temperance, glaring at the waiter. He appeared to feel Temperance's eyes because he moved his attention between her and James as he objected to James' request.

Temperance sat high in her chair, while glaring at the waiter. "It is a little warm in here," she thought. Temperance took her jacket off and dropped it to the floor.

"What is this?" the waiter wondered. "Isn't the family concerned by one of their party disrobing in public?"

Temperance adjusted her seat and moved her powerful fluke onto the seat of her chair, bent under her rump. The waiter fell back. He dropped the tray of glasses and rubbed his eyes. He saw Temperance sitting nude from the waist up.

Mary watched Temperance stare at the waiter. He was totally unnerved. He began to stutter his speech as he stooped to clear the broken glass from the floor. He looked straight at Temperance's fish tail. She adjusted, moving it down from her chair.

When he had gathered his service items, he arose staring at Temperance with a terribly disturbed look upon his face. "Yes, of course," the waiter mumbled. "We will bring the children their dinner, as you requested," the unnerved waiter said. He stumbled away as if he could not find control of his feet.

"Yes, as for us, we will be having the daily special along with our wee friends outside," James said when the waiter returned.

"Yes, of course," the waiter said, as he hurried away from the table.

"Is he a bleedin' Englishman too, James?" William asked when he left the table side.

"Seems like they all are, brother," James said. "The Irish here had better learn to hide their roots from the light of day. That goes for you too, Mr. Songbird," James said.

"A man could make a living renting English Boler hats around here," William said. "But then, it would have to be with rent due up front." James and Mary laughed at William's joke. William was right. It was either laugh or cry.

Their meals arrived with the waiter, and he placed them before them. James gave Mary and William a look, as he kept his hands folded in his lap and stared at the waiter.

A few minutes later, the waiter returned with a tray and two plates that he took to the porch and the pair of street kids, still peering through the glass. They looked up, and through the window at James, William, Temperance and Mary with a broad smile and a mouth full of chicken and noodles. The girl put her wee thumb up, as a gesture of thanks. Her four new friends around the table raised theirs in return.

James, William, Mary and Temperance finished their meal and paid the waiter. "We are rooms 4 and 6. We would appreciate it if you would be so kindly to remember us in the future as paying guests in this establishment, and not do us the dishonor of questioning our ability to pay our keep," James scolded.

"Yes, of course," he said, looking nervous over the confrontation.

"If you do, I might leave you some change for yourself. It is up to you, but you can throw the brake on your Irish insults, if you know what is good for you. James went on, "Every time we sit down in here and those two children are out there looking through the window, they will be our guests. Can you understand that man?" James asked.

The waiter nodded his head and William raised his thumb at the little girl smiling through the window.

They walked through the door and onto the boardwalk, past the two street kids who were finishing the noodles and bread. "How were your chicken noodles, children," James asked.

"Yummmmm," the young girl replied. "Thank you sir," the little boy said. "And thank you ladies too."

"Where do you children live?" Mary asked.

"Over there." She pointed at the pile of rags at the end of the boardwalk.

"Out here?" Mary asked. "Out here in the weather?" she repeated. "Where are your parents?" Mary continued her questioning.

"I don't know," the little girl said. "I think they are in heaven," she went on. "They took to the coughing fever," the young boy replied.

"Oh my," Mary said. "James!" she said.

"Yes, Mary. Just a moment," James said.

James went back into the dining room and talked to the waiter. He pointed to the group outside looking through the window. Temperance stood on the street, naked at the chest glaring at the waiter. James and William were unaware of the waiter's distress.

The waiter began to nod his head to whatever James was saying to him.

James returned to the anxious group and said," Children, when you are done with your meal, please take your plates into the nice waiter in the dining room. He will arrange a room for the two of you. You will not have to sleep on the street any longer."

"And," Mary said.

"And, you can have your meals inside everyday, as well," James continued. "Please mind your manners while you are in the dining room."

"Mary and Miss Temperance will take you two over to the dry goods store to buy some clothes," James concluded. "See you in the morning for breakfast."

The walks in store fronts were covered with overheads that advertised the shop's businesses, lined along the streets.

They left the two street kids perched under the shade of one, enjoying their meal. Over their heads, a sign read, "Help wanted, Wait staff," next to it was a much bigger one, "NO IRISH NEED APPLY."

James walked out and met a young man and woman, begging in the street. "How long have ya' been in port, sir?" James asked."

"Two days sir, we spent almost every cent we had getting here. Then we were met by a big man when we came down the ship ramp. He took our bags and took us to Shanty Town, at the edge of the city and demanded what little money we had left. Now we are penniless, but we got away from the Irish housing. There are hundreds of families there, and they do not look happy. We left as soon as we could escape," he said."

"Well, let's see what we can do about that. Come with me," James instructed. William stood by shaking his head at his stubborn older brother. "Now who's acting up?" he thought. William could remember a number of times when people peeved James by telling him what he can do and could not do. "James was not a man to be trifled with," he thought. He had a slow fuse, but once he was riled, someone was going to pay.

James had the couple, each one on his arm as he walked to the dry good store. "Oh, boy," William said.

"What is he up to William?" Mary asked.

"He's about to convert a couple of Irishmen," William answered.

He re-entered the dry goods store to the surprise of the clerk. "These fine people will be needin' six dresses for the lady, and four pants and shirts for the gentleman, along with shoes and hats for both," James demanded.

The clerk scurried around the store until she had a pile of clothes, shoes and hats at the counter.

"And the total will be".........James waited while the clerk added up the sum due.

"Three and forty," she said.

"OK folks, get on your clothes on and meet me in front of the boarding house café. We'll be filling jobs for our English innkeeper today," James said.

James, William, Temperance and Mary stood on the edge of the street as the pair of newly dressed Englishmen came across the street with a broad smile on their faces.

"Ya' look great, don't they Mary?" William offered.

"They surely do!" Mary agreed.

"I forgot to ask your names, folks," James said.

We are Maggie and David Buckalew," the man said.

"Scots are ya' then?" William asked.

"Scots, we are," David said. "Our folks came to Ireland from the Scottish Highlands many years ago, looking for a better life," David continued.

"OK, fine. Now you're English. Let's go," James said. He motioned to them to follow him in to speak to the innkeeper.

"David and Maggie, follow me and don't ask questions," James said as he took the "Help Wanted. No Irish need Apply" sign down from the door with more authority than was needed, but James had enough of this nonsense.

"Yes sir," David said, not looking to disagree with a determined James.

They entered the café with the sign in hand and gave it to the innkeeper. "Ya' won't be needin' this now," James said.

"And why would that be?" the waiter asked. He looked like he had seen enough of James today, but did not dare cross him and that mysterious black haired, fish woman again.

"Mr. and Mrs. Buckalew here, are friends of mine from London. They ran a café there. They'll do just fine in the kitchen," James said without allowing the inn keeper to react. "I suggest that they work for room and board only, for the first week," James explained. "Then you can pay them a decent wage at the end of that week, if they work out for you."

"How's that for a deal?" James asked.

"Actually, not too bad," the waiter said. "I have been looking for some qualified folks to help out here. I can't get any one but......Ir......

"You are Buckalew," not Bucceleuch, the Jacobite Scots from the Scottish highlands?"

"No, of course not," Buckalew lied.

"Well, my family and I could always take our two month's rent and board somewhere else if that would bring ya' a little more comfort," James said, approaching the point of intolerance from this English chump.

"Or do we need to stand around while ya' pick the fly poop out of the pepper?" James asked.

"No. I think that these are good enough arrangements for all of us," the waiter said.

"If they're English, they are good enough for me," he said, as he took them to the back room and they began their new employment.

"Well now," James said, his face beginning to show his impatience with the man. "We are pleased that you have made sure to only hire your own."

"Ok," Maggie said, "Let's go to work."

"One more thing for us, please," James said.

"Yes, anything," Mr. Buckalew said.

"Did you notice those two little urchins on the front stoop when we came in?" James asked.

"Yes, as a matter of fact we did," Mrs. Buckalew answered.

"We have arranged to pay for their room and board," James explained. "They are homeless orphans. If you could see fit to care, and look over them, we would all be eternally grateful."

"Consider it done," Mrs. Buckalew said. She brought the children in from the stoop and took them to their room.

"Thank you," James said.

"No sir. Thank you." Mr. Buckalew said.

He went to the basin and pile of pots and began washing.

There was a bath house and the dry good store that James and William used earlier today. There was also a livery, across the street. They crossed the roadway, busy with carriages and wagons of all shapes and sizes delivering and loading freight in both directions. They walked into the livery and found the stable master brushing a pair of large draft horses.

"Good morning to ya," he said. "How can I help you?"

"We will be needin' two pair to pull our wagon south," James said, not attempting to hide his Irish brogue.

"Where are ya' from lad?" the man asked.

"I am not sure I should tell you'………the way people are treated here," William said. "And what difference does it make, anyway?" William asked.

"Just here, from Belfast," James finally answered, pulling William aside.

"I thought that I recognized your brogue lad," the man said. "I'm from

Belfast and Londonderry me' self. I've been here for three years now. I left right after the English laid siege to Londonderry.

"Well, you'll be pleased to know that your home boys broke the siege and chased poor King James out of town. The bleedin' traitor," William said

"How did it go, then lad," the livery man asked?

"Well, it seems that they broke the siege on the river with an English boat, no less, and took the people out of Londonderry and freed them. King James fled the country. I am not sure where he went. He surely didn't stay in Ireland, and even the Scots don't want him back, and the English never did want him," William said. "Yellow as rag weed, that one."

"How did you get your business started, being from Belfast, and the way they treat the Irish around here," James said.

"Oh, I was fortunate. Some of our countrymen come off o' these boats lookin' like they have been years crossin'," The man said. "Sean Gallagher, is the name," he said, and extended his hand to James. "Proud to know ya' son."

"That, they do Sean," James said, as he extended his own hand. "James Thomson is the name, and this is my wife Mary, formerly Mary Towes from County Antrim, and my brother, William, the rude one here. And this young lady is Temperance Brickey."

"Me, rude?" if that's not the donkey callin' the horse an ass," William replied.

Gallagher continued his gaze on Temperance.

"And where are you from Miss?" Gallagher asked Temperance.

"Belfast and Ballyhalbert," she said.

"I thought that might be so," Gallagher said. "Are you among the 'Black Irish?" Gallagher asked.

Temperance did not answer him. She only stared at him.

"I mean no offense Madam," Gallagher said as he saw William look in disbelief at what he had just asked Temperance.

"The 'Black Irish' are among the miracle workers of the northern shores of Ulster. They have special powers among sea faring people and villages like Ballyhalbert," Gallagher finished. He dropped the subject when he realized that Temperance knew what was being asked.

"Ulsters, you all are now?" he finally said in an exaggerated brogue.

"Our father ran a black smith trade in Belfast. He was good enough to save for our passage, but not healthy enough to share it with us."

Yep' my folks had a farm in County Antrim," Gallagher said. "They once lived in a small fishing village on the coast of County Down and County Antrim. They were run out of their farm by a bunch of English lackeys who intended to run the place. It seems like they bit off more than they could chew, because they let it go and never really made much of it."

"The conditions here are bad for an Irishmen, particularly Catholic Irish," Gallagher said. "They seem to put as many out of their misery as they deliver ashore," he continued. "They either starve or die from ship borne disease. I would not be surprised if they don't begin to quarantine these boats before they come ashore. Before long they will, unless something is done."

"People here are becoming intolerant of so much sickness coming ashore," Gallagher added.

"Too many of the people in this town forget where they come from and who they are. Many of us came off of boats just like these folks, but they get their nose in the air now that they are so well situated. Now they live off of the sweat of others," he said.

"Mr. Penn and Mr. Spotswood, pay for many of them and then cart them off for a few years servitude. Then they may be allowed to join the move south. They are beginning to talk about lands at the end of the Shenandoah Valley and into Botetourt, County, Richmond has its own port," Sean said. "For now, I sell a few horses and stable the rest."

"I have been very fortunate," Gallagher went on. "The poor folks in Shanty Town live miserable lives, but they are making things much worse for themselves. The drinking, hootin' and hollerin' and the thieving is doing them no good. The Irish are hated here, and they are not helping their own situation a bit," Gallagher said.

"The best thing for an Irishman to do, assuming that he's not dead when he gets here, is escape from port as quickly as possible. Unfortunately, those that work in the hands of their contract owners are much better off than those who try to remain free. We are not doing ourselves any good, here," Sean said. "The faster the Irish can leave here, the better. The sooner they can turn their backs on Philadelphia and the English snobs who run it, the better."

"The longer this goes on," Gallagher continued as his voice began to show the emotion he had for this issue, "the worse this is going to get. The Irish from Shanty Town come down to the pier and around town everyday. In the beginning they asked for work, politely. They are not so polite anymore."

"Philadelphia is already filled with street people," Sean went on. Settlement leaders can not build housing fast enough to handle these people, and to be truthful, they probably should not," Sean said. "The Irish need to move on. They will continue to be in jeopardy if they stay here.

"Being independent here in the colonies," Gallagher went on, getting louder as he continued, "is not going to serve these stubborn Irishmen well. When they arrive here they do not help each other and they do not learn anything from one family to another. If they would only help each other when they land at port, a lot of this could be avoided, but these stubborn people trust no one. If and when they ever get on the wagon road south, they will need to cooperate with each other. They will really need each other then. The Irish need to put their damned independent spirits down and learn to help each other," he said.

"What of the road, then Sean? What is it like?" James asked.

"Well, through all of Pennsylvania, until they reach the Potomac River, it is heavily forested. The trail served the Iroquois Indians who needed nothing more than a trail through the forest. They hunted for game as they went and had no reason for a larger road," Sean said. "They were afoot, and it suited them just fine."

"When settlers began to need a way to travel between the mountain ranges, hauling everything that we use to set up a farm, we needed the path wider and suitable for wagons," Sean continued. "The more we decided to haul, the bigger the wagons got to be. The bigger the wagon, the bigger the horses," he finally concluded.

"Would you be looking for a two pair to pull your Conestoga down that road, Sean finally asked?"

"Yes, we are having a wagon built in Mr. Kreigler's shop, down the street."

"He's a good wagon maker. Not much for conversation, but he is good at what he does," Sean said. "His wagons are made of oak and other native hardwoods. They make the best wagons, and his iron pieces he gets from O'Leary, down the way, there. Once he has your wagon done, it will probably out live all of us, and our grandchildren too."

"The way they treat the Irish here, I can understand that." William said. James turned and looked at William who was about to get Gallagher restarted.

"Well, that is true. But there is always another side of the coin. That may help us understand their point of view, as much as I would like to avoid it. English investors, put a lot of money into this settlement to get it started. They have been expecting a return on their money for many years now. Unfortunately, their brethren over there keep putting poor, unskilled Irish folks on these ships, instead of skilled craftsmen who can make a contribution. The only thing us Irishmen can make is whisky. They can't work at anything and they are half dead when they get, Sorry ladies," Gallagher said, remembering Mary and Temperance behind him. "Mary turned away and began watching the people moving about on the street.

"Anyway, Gallagher said, in a hushed tone, "the English empty their poor houses, jails and orphanages onto these boats instead of sending craftsmen, like yourselves. It is an ugly situation that only gets worse every year. Some come over, and like I said, are taken to a farm to work off their servitude contract. Others spend every schilling they have and end up in Shanty Town, where you could make a cent, unless, ya made whisky, that is. Ya' never know what will happen with that. As we say," Even a black hen occasionally lays a white egg."

"They would be much better off if they took a servitude contract for a few years. Many owners give their servants a good send off at the end of their contract. Some have a wagon and a team. Some of these owners are not bad people. The problem is that the Irish do not want to trust anyone, so they loose the good with the bad," Gallagher went on.

"Many of them," Gallagher continued, are Irishmen themselves. They once came ashore without knowing anyone themselves. There are some undoubtedly bad ones, but not all of them," he went on. "Shanty Town is crawling with disease and criminals that came from London jails. They can't make a living here and do not have the means to move on either."

"Where is Shanty Town, Gallagher," James asked. "It's out west of town, easy to find. Go west until ya' smell the sour mash, and then south until ya' step in it, "he mused.

"Anyway, back to your team. I can find you two sturdy pair that you can have for fifty pounds a bit. Are ya' having an eight meter or a ten?

"We will do with an eight," James said.

"Since you are a fine lad from me' home town," Gallagher mocked, "I will throw in the tack from Bandy's tack shop down the way, here. Poor devil, he was a saddle maker by trade, making saddles for all of those fancy English ladies. Now he has not made a saddle in years. They keep him so busy making tack for wagons and their teams. He might make a saddle backwards if he ever gets to one," Gallagher laughed.

"We have employment with Kreigler for the month or so that it will take to get our wagon, James said."

"Well, you tell ole' Schmidt there that I have two pair of fine horses that will be waiting for his wagon. He does not need to worry over that," Gallagher said. "Nice to have met you Thompson. Come by and see me to let me know how things are going."

"That's T H O M S O N, no "P." William corrected.

"Well you might as well get used to the "P" son, because that name is one of the most common names in England, and they gave you a "P" whether you like it or not. You might as well get some benefit from not looking too Scottish or Irish around here. English, are ya' now?" Thompson with a "P", he said. "Nothing like a new buckle on an old shoe," he went on.

"People of Philadelphia here are quite sensitive to name spellings and family history's in trying to avoid the Scot-Irish, aren't they, Gallagher," William said. "The hotel manager just asked some folks if they were Jacobite Scots when he heard their name."

"Yes they are, no doubt," Gallagher said. "My own name is known in Ulster and has some rather ugly history with the English as well. It seems best for any people of Scot-Irish history to move on, and out of Philadelphia as soon as they can. People's history here will continue to be an issue as long as the English are in charge."

They returned from their walk around the street and went into their rooms, earlier than normal.

"This had been an exhausting day," James said.

In the morning they went to the café, dining room for some soda bread and tea. In their place they found a menu of pork, bread and eggs. Mary ordered tea and bread. She skipped the heavier dose of pork and eggs.

At seven o'clock, sharp, James and William were at Kriegler's wagon shop ready for work. They could easily sense that Old Man Kreigler was watching their every move.

Hockensmith told them where the black smith shop was and instructed them to take the wagon and get a load of iron goods and bring them back. They hitched the team from the shop and drove off in the wagon. "This must be one of the wagons that Mr. Kreigler made in the shop," William said, as they entered into the morning traffic of wagons coming and going on the street, making early morning deliveries.

When they arrived at the black smith shop they took in the sight before they entered. "Look much the same as Pa's shop, don't you think James," William asked.

"Sure does, William. The same furnace, except ours did not use the black chunks like they do here," James said.

They entered the shop to find a large man standing over his anvil as he worked on a piece of red hot iron with his tong and anvil. Sparks flew from the piece every time the man brought his hammer down upon the piece.

After a few moments, the man noticed them and asked what they needed. "Another German," William said to himself.

"We're from Mr. Kreigler's shop. He said that you may have a pick up for us this morning," James said.

As the man walked away, hopefully to get the materials that Mr. Kreigler needed, James and William looked more about the shop. The tools of the trade were hung neatly around the shop. Bellows, tongs and hammers of all kinds were hung neatly.

William saw a hinge, much like the ones he was familiar with. As the man returned, he took the piece from William and put it down, where it had been. "This way, please" He said.

James and William followed the man to a side door where they were met by a black man who was removing iron straps from a barrel. Neither James nor William had not seen a black man before. They began to sense the discomfort that their staring caused. They soon joined in, taking the straps from the barrel and placing them in their wagon. The black man said nothing as they finished loading. Neither did they.

The wagon that he and William drove was made of heavy oak planks that they got from the mill on the outskirts of town. Workers, in the shop, steamed them before bending them to the right shape. William helped a worker bend some that would be used for the curved floor of the wagon. This would keep cargo from moving around on rough roads.

James took a drill and bit and pre-drilled screw holes for hinges and straps that held the pieces together. This made it much easier to secure the pieces. The oak was much too hard to takes screws without pre-drilling holes.

James and William were busy at Kriegler's shop. Temperance wanted to go to the pier. She decided to satisfy her curiosity over Shanty Town and began a walk towards the west. As Gallagher had said, the further she walked the more obvious it was that she was going in the right direction.

Mary first noted the noise of children playing in the street and then the yelling from within the quarters. As she finally walked onto the edge of Shanty Town she was shocked to see what terrible conditions that these people lived in.

As soon as she stopped walking and stared, several people came off from their front steps and walked towards her. Mary's heart sunk as the group of toughs stood in front of her. "Can we help you with something Miss, or are you just here, in all of your finery to gawk at us," one of them said.

"I came here to see,...to.see for myself what people have told me," she stuttered, in her nervousness.

"Well, what do ya' see then?" he asked.

"I see people who need help," Mary answered. "But I am not sure how I can do that."

"You can give us some money Madam," he said. "We need money," he continued.

"I don't have a lot of money, but that may not be the best thing for you anyway. You need employment and you need a way to get out of Philadelphia. There are men at port everyday looking to pick up workers from ships coming ashore, even that is better than having your wives and children live like this," Mary said.

She looked around the menacing looking tough that stood before her. There were lines of clapboard shacks with simple wooden steps that led to a door. A single window stood by each door. Most of those windows had women and children peering out through them to Mary and the group of ten or twelve young men. They seemed to be anticipating something that they did want to miss.

Wash pails sat out front, by the step, filled with what appeared to be dirty wash water. Trash was strewn about that groups of men stood in groups drinking from bottles that they passed around.

Mary soon realized that she had made a big mistake coming here alone. James would be very upset, she realized, if he knew that she were here. "How am I to get away," she thought in a panic. These men do not want to hear what I have to say, and they are taking my curiosity poorly.

To her surprise, Mary saw Temperance approaching from down the street. The street toughs that were assailing Mary also saw her approaching.

"Hey, look at this lass, will you boys," one of them said.

Mary's hart jumped at the relief that Temperance's appearance caused, but she wondered how Temperance would handle this matter.

The boys surrounded Temperance and began to speak to her. Mary could not hear the discussion, but she saw the confidence on Temperance's face as she stood, her arms crossed before her assailants.

After a short time, the boys took several steps back. Then, they suddenly turned around and quickly left. They crossed the road and took up their positions that they held when Mary first arrived.

Mary watched them as they stood staring at Temperance, as if they had seen a ghost.

Temperance walked to Mary, took her arm and began walking her away.

Just as they turned to leave, a city policeman came around the corner on his horse. When he saw Mary and Temperance, he came towards them immediately. "Madam.... Madam, is there a problem here. What are you ladies doing here?" he asked.

"This is no place for the likes of you ladies. Now be on your way," he commanded.

Mary had no intention of telling James when she saw him. She realized that her curiosity and her stubborn idealism had gotten her into trouble, and she needed to keep this to herself.

On the way back to town, Mary asked Temperance, "What did you say to those boys to get them to leave us alone?"

"Oh, some of them came from the same region of Ireland that I came from. They decided that that did not need anything from the two of us," Temperance explained.

"Well, I don't know what you said but you must have scared the stuffin' out of them. Did you see the look on their faces?" Mary asked.

"I guess I didn't," Temperance answered.

Mary brought a lunch around for James and William. She looked like one of the many women they saw on the street with their bonnets and straw baskets on their arms as they went from shop to shop. She had bread, cheese and boiled meat. Mary should the boys how to put the meat in the middle of the split bread and make a sandwich. "A sandwich, is it?" William said. Must be named after some Englishman............or a German," William said quietly.

"Mary, I keep thinking about what Sean, the livery worker said about the load of Irish coming off of these ships every week, James said. "He said that those that accept a decent servitude contract are much better off in the end than those who try to live on their own and end up in Shanty Tow, James continued.

"The problem then is that there is no one to talk to them when they first set foot on the dock," Mary said.

"That's right, Mary," James continued. "Those that are fortunate like we are can afford to pay for our services. Those that are taken off to work on a farm are much better off than those who stubbornly try to remain independent. They apparently are set free at the end of their contract and can join others going down the wagon road."

"Shanty Town is ruining everyone's view of the Irish. As it grows, the problem only gets worse. Eventually it will erupt into street riots," James said.

"Are you saying that you think that I can help new arrivals by directing them in the right direction," Mary asked?

"It certainly is not something that anyone else has done," James said, "and I can't help but feel that the Irish will turn sour on America before they get a chance to see what it has to offer," James continued.

"I am not sure what I can do, but I will see. I have been around town this morning, Mary said. "I can not get used to all of the shops that are here," she went on. It is so different from what we are used to. There are shop owners make investments here. In Belfast they were barely hanging on as it continues to decline," Mary said.

"There is a bake shop over there, where I bought these loaves, and a dress shop, dry goods store, and probably more that I have not seen yet. "This butter and cheese came from the creamery around the corner," she continued.

"I am happy that you bought these dresses for us. Most women are wearing this same style and it helps me blend in," Mary said. "They are different from the home made ones we used to wear in Belfast. They all seem to wear the same hats and laced boots, as well,: she went on.

"There are some shops on the back streets as well," Mary said. There are a couple of laundries, and grocers and taverns.

Chapter X

As the days went on, James, Mary, Temperance and William minded their own business and pretty much kept to themselves. They took their meals in the café, at the boarding house. David and Maggie Buckalew still worked in the kitchen and on several occasions they were met there by the children that they had provided meals for before.

They had been taken in by the Buckalews and were regulars around the inn and dining room where they helped the Buckalews with clearing tables. They always got kind words of appreciation from the children.

"When I see them, I always think of how fortunate the three of us have been," James said. "Our folks sacrificed to save enough for us to live above the fray here in the colonies. Makes one wonder what they really knew about the conditions here," he went on. "We were fortunate because father's business kept them above the fray in Belfast as well. We did nothing to deserve the difference between us and all of the other Irish her, we were just blessed with fortune."

James and William had been saving their money for supplies that they would be needin' on the road. Mr. Hockensmith let them keep these items near their work space, where carpenters were working on their wagon. They had canteens, barrels, axes, knives, and picks that they had made on their own time.

William and James bought a pair of rifles that were made by a craftsman in Lancaster, Pennsylvania. They also purchased lead and a mold to make the bullets. Gun powder and packing supplies would be picked up later. They had heard that game was plentiful on the trail. If that was the case, they thought, it would not be necessary to take a lot of dried meat pemmican along with them.

Mary shopped for blankets, extra clothing and a few pieces of dining ware that they would use once they arrived at their destination. They had been given a map by Sean Gallagher, the livery man. They studied the road marked on it with great interest.

"The Great Philadelphia Wagon Road," was clearly marked on the chart paper, showing it traveling along a long valley that worked its way across the Potomac and down to the narrow valley, just east of the Appalachian Mountains and west of the Blue Ridge Mountains. There were a few alternate paths marked on the chart but they almost all worked their way down to the Carolina territories, near Richmond. It showed the Catawba path, the Old Kittanning Indian Trail, Braddock's road, Tupehocken Path, The Great Shamokin Path, Forbes road and a few others that stretched from the North, near New York through the Carolinas.

At the dinner table that night, William told Mary and James that he and Temperance had talked about their future. "We have decided to be married and find our place in the Carolina territory along the seaboard. Temperance would like to live near the shore, as she did as a child. I understand that there is still coastal and available there.

"That is great news," Mary said.

"Welcome to our family, Temperance," Mary said.

There was a small ceremony the following day, they were all anxious to strike out on their own. Since they did not have a plan to follow, they had no real idea where they would end up. None of them seemed to care. One looked as good as another, as long as it lead them out of Philadelphia and its overcrowded streets.

Beggars were everywhere. One did not venture out at night for the fear of being mugged by people who appeared to be beyond hope. They lived in despair, crowded into small tenant shacks in Shanty Town. The men drank themselves to sleep every night while the women tried to pacify their hungry children by keeping their minds on something besides their empty stomachs.

Make shift buildings, tattered and torn by the traffic of homeless people who had fought their way in and out of Shanty Town were everywhere. Children played in the street, near naked from lack of decent clothes. Men and women sat on ragged porch stoops watching the more fortunate go by.

Their future would not change their plight until the American Civil War came along and took their men out of these ghettos as conscripts. They would bolster the enlistments for the Union Army that was having trouble filling their ranks. Thanks to the law that gave wealthy people the ability to pay three hundred dollars to fulfill their requirement. Expendable Irishmen would take their place.

"Most of these people would never leave Shanty Town, James said. "The longer that they stay, the less likely that it will be can escape the poverty and class discrimination that takes away their hope."

"The Irish are looked down upon and kept in their place by Philadelphia's inability to provide a means to take them in and make them productive," James went on. "They are kept together in Shanty Town and out of the view of people of means who might want to set up business in the district or invest in another."

There were a few, well-to-do people that came off of the ships among the mass of Irish that came from below deck spilling out onto the docks, creating as scene everyday. They were given no direction from ship crews. Their destiny would be determined by the thugs that stood at the bottom of the ramp. Some would be taken away to their owner, some would find their way to Shanty Town after what little money they had was taken by men who grabbed at their bags and charged them ridiculous fees to deliver them to the outskirts of town.

Organizers continued to look for skilled trades people on the boats, but got more Irish from London's jails and poor houses. Some children were unloaded as well. They were destined for an estate or farm and used as house servants, stable boys or garden labor until they satisfied the demands of their contracts. They were taken away and out of sight from those who might look too closely.

Mary visited the pier one late morning when an immigrant ship came into port. Like the one that se, James and William arrived on, it came from

Belfast. She stood back as the ship was secured to the pier and the crew made ready to let passengers off.

The air was stiff with anxiety as passengers pushed against the rails trying to get their first view of Philadelphia. Finally, a ramp was attached and passengers began to boil over the pier in near panic.

Mary stayed back and watched as people scrambled down the ramp trying to get away from the ship and its memories, while in some cases still trying to hold onto their children and family members. It was easy to see what James described as the utter chaos of this scene, Mary thought. The majority of the crowd, Mary thought, appeared to have no idea what was expected of tem or what they were required to do. This majority seemed stunned and there pushing one direction and then another trying to understand their circumstance made the crowd reach near panic.

As time went on, Mary saw a few people being taken away. These could be contracted servants going to their farm to serve out their time, or they could be people that were being taken away to Shanty town. Mary thought that it was difficult to tell. A few walked away from the dock and into town like she' James and William had done. The one thing that was obvious, Mary thought is that there was no organization to this at all. There were no officials offering assistance, that was obvious, Mary said to herself.

After an hour, the crowd had eased along with the tension that filled the air first upon arrival, Mary thought. Then she saw one family standing off to the side with the look of desperation upon their faces.

Mary walked to them and said, "Sorry, excuse me, but, you seem like you need assistance. May I help you?"

At first the mother pulled her two children closer to her and then looked off to her husband who had his back to Mary. He looked off into one direction then in another.

"My name is Mary Thompson, my husband and a brother-in-law just arrived a month ago, and I can certainly understand your concern since there is no one to tell passengers what they are to do. The woman said nothing. She stood in her home spun dress, dirty and tattered from the long journey.

"My name is Mary Thompson," she repeated. "We just arrived from

Belfast last month." Is this ship from Belfast?" Mary asked as she stepped a little closer to the woman and her children.

Then, Mary was frightened as the husband turned in towards her, and reached for the children who were still attached to their mother.

"I am truly sorry, Madam, Sir," Mary began. "But we were in a similar state when we arrived last month and I understand your concern over not knowing what to do," she said.

"I understand the panic of this moment and would like to help you if you will allow," she said, still no one said anything. Then the little girl asked," Madam, where are we?"

"Well, this is Philadelphia, and you have just arrived in America, Mary said as she reached to pat the child on her face. Her mother grabbed the child and turned away from Mary, while the husband stepped between Mary and his wife and daughter.

"I am trying to help you" Mary said.

"We do not know you and we do not need your help," the man said. He turned his wife and children away and began walking towards town center. Mary was shocked and bewildered by this event. She felt terrible about trying to help these people and have them think that she was somehow going to harm them. Mary stood with her back to the ship and the scene of people milling about trying to understand their circumstances.

Just as she was about to walk off and return to town, down hearted by this morning's events, she heard a small voice say," Excuse me, Madam."

When she turned, she was face to face with a young couple and a small boy.

"Excuse us, Madam, we just arrived and have no idea where we are or what we are to do. You don't seem to be part of this, and we were hoping that you could perhaps assist us," the woman said. Mary's heart jumped at the suddenness of the moment.

"We just arrived," the young woman repeated. "We hoped that you could help us find an inn where we can rest," the woman said.

"Certainly," Mary finally managed to say. "We were in the same condition when we arrived last month. I am sorry, but this scene is so terrible to witness. I am still shocked by the way people are unloaded into this city," Mary said.

"Yes, sorry. My name is Mary Thompson, we came from Belfast last month. We needed an inn when we first arrived. Are you contracted to a farm or enterprise operated by the settlement's organizers, Mary asked?

"No," The man said. "We are hoping to move out of the city and we understand that there is a road that will take us to southern territories. We will look for a place of our own," the man said firmly.

"That is good," Mary said, "Because, we Irish have been hard for this city to absorb and I am afraid that they are not used to our ways," Mary concluded. "Most of the city's organizers are English.

"My husband had us pick up some new clothes at the dry goods store in town," Mary pointed up the street towards town center, "He thought it best that we get rid of the clothes that we wore for a month before we introduced ourselves to this city," she said. "I would suggest you do the same, before you do anything else, even though I know that you need rest."

"I am afraid that the more you can afford to separate yourselves from this port scene the better your beginning in colonies will go," Mary went on. "If you can pay cash for you stay at the inn, and offer it up front so that the clerks concern is addressed from the beginning, you will be better received.

"Please do not allow anyone to direct you," and then Mary realized what she was about to say. "I think that you would be well served by staying away from the housing area that natives call Shanty Town," Mary said.

"They have had a terrible time with the Irish that end up in Shanty Town. The rents are extremely high and the conditions are almost poisonous. You would be better served to stay in town at an inn if you can and begin making preparations for living this city as soon as possible."

"You are truly blessed," Mary said. You are truly fortunate to have the means to leave this city as soon as possible. My husband and brother-in-law have located a wagon maker and a livery operation that have worked out well for us. They are both down this way," Mary pointed up the street again. On the second street," she finished. "My husband and brother-in-law are now working at the wagon shop and you may ask for them if you would like their help," Mary said.

"Sorry, the young woman offered. We are John and Megan Lochmatomy, from County Antrim. We do appreciate your kindness and concern.

"You are welcome and please forgive me for intruding like this. It is just that my husband, and his brother and I have been so blessed by things that we really had nothing to do with and it is very disturbing to see people treated like they are," Mary hurried to explain. "We have been blessed, and we believe that we can help those that are in the situation that we would have been had it not been for the generosity of his parents," Mary finished.

"Thank you, Mary," Megan said, as they turned to go into the city.

As Mary returned to the pier for ship arrivals she began to notice the absence of chaos that had previously marked the scene at port. There was less agony and distress being displayed as people came off of the ships. The pushing and shoving had been replaced with the appearance of a sense of hope.

Many new arrivals made their way towards the small office on the pier. They gathered around a woman who was addressing them about something that they obviously needed to hear about. As Mary approached closer, she saw Temperance standing on a crate, speaking to the crowd.

"If you have the ability to leave this town," Mary heard her say, "you should get your supplies and move on. Our kind is not wanted here."

"Stay away from the place they call, "Shanty Town." It is a trap," Temperance continued, "You would be better to sign on as an indentured servant for three years than to find yourself trapped there."

Temperance saw Mary standing in the back and motioned her to the front. "This lady and I, and our husbands arrived here a month or so ago and were faced with the same problem that some of you now find yourselves," she said.

"Servitude is a better form of bondage than what our fellow Irish experience in Shanty Town. There is no employment here," she concluded.

Mary saw the toughs that frequented the pier standing in the back, away from the crowd. They stood with an inquisitive look that Mary had seen on others in Temperance's presence. "They had the same look as those boys at Shanty Town had when they were confronted by Temperance," Mary realized.

"How long have you been doing this?" Mary asked.

"This is my second day," Temperance answered. "I hated to see these poor people in the hands of those thugs in the back."

"Well, I see," Mary said. "But how have you kept them at bay when you take their lively hoods?" Mary asked.

"I simply impressed upon them the need to avoid laying hands on news arrivals," Temperance answered, as she took Mary's hand and helped her down from the crate that they had been standing upon.

"Let's go," Temperance said. "We are done here, for today."

Chapter XI

As the middle of the second month in Philadelphia approached, the livery man showed James and William two fine pair of matching draft horses. They were bred especially for the heavy Conestoga wagons that would be their burden for months to come. James and William had found their way around Kreigler's shop pretty well.

Although nothing was ever mentioned, Mr. Kreigler no longer watched over them as he did when they first appeared. Had he been able to permanently employ them he would have, regardless of the sign on the front of his shop.

James was becoming a fine rigger, adding the final hardware to the wagon and fitting the bowed pieces of strap lumber that they used as ribs to hold the canvas in place over the wagon's bed.

William supervised a group of women who worked at the difficult task of sewing the heavy white canvas together that would make up the cover. This was terrible, hard labor for anyone, let alone a woman. The canvas was heavy, and over time worked the skin off of their fingers as they stitched in the loops that would take the ribs when the wagon was finished.

William helped James apply the hinges and iron straps that held the wagons together. They were both good with their large hands that had been strengthened by years of work in their father's blacksmith shop.

Mary had told James about her first day at the pier and about finding Temperance there directing new arrivals. It had had a great affect on her,

James noticed. She had made herself vulnerable by offering her help and it had been met with a strong rebuff in the beginning. She had been saved within a few moments after that first tragic interchange, and it thankfully had restored her positive frame of mind. He was also glad that Temperance was there with her.

Mary had a special gift, James thought. She lived vulnerably. She always offered herself to others without much concern for herself. She was one of the people that the rest of us meet in life that people flock to with their own concerns in mind. Mary had a nurturing love for people and somehow they could see it. She was truly a special person, James thought. This world could use a lot more like her, he thought.

Having come from humble beginnings, Mary recognized life's blessings when they came to her life. Her parents have been ruined when English Protestants came to take away her land. They were reduced to working day work when they could find it. Her father had died first, and her mother followed soon thereafter.

Immigrating to America to escape the problems in Ireland never occurred to Mary's mother. Her escape came at the end of her life in Ireland and upon this earth. It had placed so many burdens upon her. She had her own escape planned and accepted it when it came to her one night in her sleep.

Mary had returned a few times to the pier since her first day. She learned that she must wait until the push of the traffic eased after arrival. To meet the crowd head on was much more than a small lady, on her own, should expose themselves to. In her way, she helped a number of people. She referred them to James and William at the shop. As a result, the Kriegler wagon business had seen an increase over the last few weeks. People came in to do business with them as they prepared to take on the Great Pennsylvania Wagon Road and the unknown beyond.

Hockensmith had finished six Conestoga wagons during the time that the Thompson brothers were there. They had contracted for 12 more thanks to Mary's referrals at the pier. Each one had been fitted with a horse team and tack that made a respectable outfit when they left the shop and began their journey down the Great Philadelphia Wagon Road.

No one ever told Hockensmith, and certainly not Mr. Kreigler, about

Mary working up business for the shop. That was not her intention, James thought, and it would probably be best to avoid that issue as they had no interest in becoming anymore attached to the shop than they already were. When it became time to leave, they wanted to be able to leave this part of their experience behind without regret.

The last few items secured for their trip, was a water barrel, food and the tack from Bandy's tack livery. In the morning they said good bye to Mr. Kreigler and Mr. Schmidt, packed their wagon.

"I have two small things that I need to get before we leave," Mary exclaimed.

"Mary," James said, "we are loaded here," She never even turned around to meet James' questioning.

James looked at Mary and scratched his head under his eight paneled news boy hat, shaking his head all the while. "Mary, Mary, what on earth have ya' done now, woman," he asked?

"Now James," she said when she returned a few minutes later," You know that you were thinking the same thing. Weren't you?"

"Yes Mary, I was," he answered. "You read my mind again, didn't you?"

"I just couldn't leave this place without relieving some of the burden that these people have in this place. We have been fortunate, and we need to share some of it with those who have no responsibility for their unfortunate fate," Mary said.

David and Maggie Buckalew came down the street with a hand cart. It had two wheels and two long arm poles to walk between as it was pulled along by hand. They had a few supplies and changes of clothing, and Thomas and Mary Katherine from the café, sitting in the middle.

"We hope that you do not mind they we come along with you," Buckalew said.

"Of course not," William said. "We would be proud to have you but we had better leave before Mary's kindness loads us up any further. She's the Pied Piper of Philadelphia."

Chapter XII

James, and Mary Towes Thompson and William and Temperance, with a new "p" to their name, struck out on the trail with their new companions, Thomas and Mary Katherine Fahey.

Thomas and Mary Katharine were brother and sister. Mary Katherine must have been a year or two older than Thomas. They had crossed in an immigrant ship from London, brought aboard by English authorities after their parents were taken to the poor house.

They were trying to get enough to pay for their crossing when they were caught taking fruit from the back side of a grocery. Their defense was that it was rubbish. Having no source of income, they were taken to the poor house. The children had lost track of their parents and ended up being taken away by a pair of policemen and eventually put aboard a ship to Philadelphia. When they arrived, they sneaked away in the clamber of the crowd.

Their first planned stop would be Lancaster, Pennsylvania. It would take six days to arrive in Lancaster, according to James interpretation of the chart that he got from Gallagher

The road was surprisingly rough, and surprisingly forested right up to the edge of the path. James thought as they began their first leg of the journey, towards Lancaster. The road was bumpy and dusty when dry and muddy when wet. Thomas and Mary Katherine rode upon the horses in the back. Their little legs could not even begin to provide a grasp of the horses, so William and James had rigged leg straps and hand reins for them to hold on to.

"So far, so good," they thought. The rough trail and wagon wheel ruts gave the extra rigging a good test. The two children bounced along on their mounts as if they were atop the world.

Just as Gallagher had said, most of the road was really a path through thick forests of trees.

The horses stumbled, as they tried to gain a footing on the road. It was rutted and uneven as it jostled Mary, sitting on the lazy board, a pull out seat board that was positioned behind the front wheel on the left side of the wagon. Conestoga wagons did not have a front bench seat.

Wagon owners either rode upon one of the horses or on the "lazy board", as it was called. This began the American custom of passing on the right side of oncoming traffic. In this way drivers could better see their way past other wagons as they me on the rode.

The Buckalews kept their cart up high, out of the road ruts and made their way through without difficulty. Thomas and Mary Katherine walked along side of the cart and helped pull when they got their cart stuck.

They traveled on and finally reached Lancaster late in the afternoon of the fifth day. They were all exhausted. James found an inn and bath house where they spent the evening leisurely bathing and resting.

On the next day they struck out for York, just beyond the shore of the Potomac River. Based on what they were told, they should be able to traverse the trail to its end in North Carolina in 75 to 125 days. From the difficulties that they ad experienced from Philadelphia to Lancaster, it may take twice as long.

As they finally approached the banks of the Potomac, they were met by several other wagons waiting to cross the river.

There was a steep, sloped bank where the trail met the river. The recent rain had swollen the river. Silt mucked up the water, making it difficult to determine how deep that water was, even close to shore.

James and William parked the wagon near the bank and struck a conversation with the crowd that had gathered around a wagon. "Good afternoon", William said.

"Good day," one of the men said.

"Is there a problem crossing?" James asked.

"Well, we don't rightly know," one said. "We have been her for two days. The rain has swollen the river, and we are not sure how deep it is at the crossing, let alone in midstream," he continued.

"I guess we are discussing who should be the first to go," one volunteered. "No one seems to want to find out by attempting the crossing first, and we have not decided what to do about it."

Mary looked around, as she stood near the wagon. She could see several of the women standing in the shade, talking and looking to see if the new arrivals would add a solution to their problem.

"Good day" Mary said as she approached the group.

"Good day," they returned. And no one said another word, apparently waiting to see if Mary offered any information. Seeing that they were not willing to offer anything, Mary turned and left to return to her wagon.

James and William stood among the group of men, near the shore. There conversation was going no further than Mary's, she thought.

Well, I do have a suggestion, William said, looking quickly towards James as if he needed permission to offer a solution. "We all need to cross, and staying here is probably not a good idea when we are not sure what the situation is with the Indians. Since we are all here together" William went on, "we should all cross in a line and watch out for each other, while we do it."

They all started nodding their heads in agreement and then it fell silent. "Who's going first?" one of them asked. Then they all looked at each other in silence.

"We'll go first then, William said.

James looked at William, in amazement, but he did not say anything contrary to William's offer.

"We will line up at the crossing with no more that ten meters between us, as we move the wagons down the steep bank. The women can ride the lazy board, and the children can ride on the horses so that we know where they are, and we will help each other down the slope until the last one is in the water," James explained.

"When we are all in stream we will line up along the wagons, on each side, as we cross. If there are problems we halt and then investigate," James concluded.

"All right," some one said. "Let's try it."

"I will get the wheel chain. Does any one else have one?" James asked.

They all looked t each other again, in silence.

James went to the wagon and told Mary what she was to do and fond his wheel chain. The children were secure upon their horses and they were ready for what ever was coming.

The wagon drivers reluctantly lined up. James look annoyed as he saw that even that task was not easy for these folks. Eventually they had two wagons in line, of the eleven wagons on the bank.

"William, this was your idea, Let's do it," James said.

James, William and Mary pulled their new dark blue wagon with red wheels and pulling stock up to the bank. The horses stopped, not anxious to go down the hill. William walked to the left side took off his shirt and tied it over the lead horse's eyes and gently worked the harness as the animal took his first step. James was at the left rear wheel, ready with his chain. If the heavy wagon started to slide and push the horses down the hill, he would be ready to place the chain in the wheel spokes to induce a locked wheel and act like a break." Hold on children," William said.

Mary held her position on the side seat as William moved the horses down the hill. As they approached mid-slope the weight of the wagon began pushing the horses and the left rear began to sway side ways. James threw his heavy chain into the wheel spokes and the wheel locked, as he hoped that it would.

Mary jumped off of the side seat and moved to safety near William. Mary looked up. Mary Katherine and Thomas were still aboard their horses and seemed to be doing well. David and Maggie's cart was tied to the rear of the new wagon while David helped in keeping the team moving.

The wagon regained its direction and slowly managed its way down the rest of the slope and into the water.

The crowd on the shore watched intently and looked at each other before they broke loose and hurried to their wagons to be the next in line. Apparently that part of the problem had been solved satisfactorily to them.

William, Temperance and Mary and the children began the crossing. The water was a hip depth for the first third of the river. So far so good,

Mary thought. Thankfully there is not a lot of current, she thought. Then the water got deeper as the reached mid point. Water was now up to Mary's hips. She cried, "William," he came over to her and placed her safely on the lead horse back. Mary looked back at James whose anxious expression change to one of thanks as he looked at William, who had the look of pride on his.

The water remained the same level as William stopped the team and looked back at James who was working the second wagon team down the slope. William saw that the others were beginning to line up, with all of the women and children on horse back.

One by one, they moved down the hill until all twelve were in the water, William moving ahead a little at a time to allow others to get in line.

They all made the crossing safely and climbed the slope on the other side. All twelve had safely navigated the crossing with no damage.

"William, slowly look to your left, upon the hill over there," James instructed. When he did he saw what had drawn James attention. There was a party of twenty or so Indians, who had apparently heard the noise from the crossing and had been watching all along.

"William, I think we should circle the wagons and stay here for the night. Let's put our backs to the river. It is going to be dark here in a bit and there is no since being caught out after dark when we don't know where we are going," James offered.

James had never really asked my opinion before, William thought. It struck William as being a little out of character for James, but he was encouraged by James' recognition.

With in an hour, the wagons were circled in a half moon shaped with the open said to the river. If any one tried to cross, they would hear it. Families built their cooking fires and a larger fire in the center where the men sat talking about the days events.

"As it was about to turn dark,………. 'James,'……….I hear someone calling. It is coming across the river. They all grabbed their rifles and lined up along the shore ready to catch the Indians in mid river. They all took a one knee position, following William's lead, aiming towards the noise coming across.

"Hold it," James said. "Hold your fire, it's a wagon. Six of ya' come with me," William said. "The rest keep an eye out."

They ran down the slope and out into the river, along side the startled family, helping them cross the river. They had two small children with them.

William and James had them move into the camp. Their horse were taken out of their harness and freed into the semi circle with the rest of them.

The family looked shocked, James thought. They explained that they were delayed and got to the river much later than they had intended. When they saw the fires on the opposite side they decided to cross. They also had noticed the Indians standing on the hill and did not want to be caught alone after dark.

During the night, the horses seemed nervous, until the group decided to put a watch near them. No doubt the Indians would love to get there hands on these horses.

The following morning they made quick work of their coffee and bacon. There were thirteen wagons and teams in the group. All seemed to understand the benefit of staying in a large group. They were on their way at day break.

The next check point was Mechanicsburg. It had been built a few years back to take advantage of the wagon traffic coming down the trail. The group pulled into the small village at supper time and lined their wagons up at the edge of town. Several men went in to town to purchase wheel chains, like the one that James used in helping them get down the slope at the river.

The next morning they were on their way to Winchester. It would take another three or four days, depending on weather and road conditions. The big wagons, built as freight haulers took the bumpy road well. Those that attempted to ride within them did not fair as well. They were made for weight and smooth roads it seemed, as stiff as a poker.

The road continued to pass through heavily forested land on the way to Winchester. They were on the look out for Indian that some had been warned about when the left Philadelphia. James had seen a few lone Indians just inside the tree line but had not said anything, since there was no benefit of upsetting everyone. He did ask William to tell the men to make sure that women and children were kept close to the wagons as they moved along. Those that could ride on horseback or the seat board probably should.

At mid day, one of the men told William that he had seen a pair of Indians in the tree line. "Keep an eye on them, but they are just waiting for an opportunity to steal a horse or woman.

The afternoon passed without event. They circled the wagons, put the horses in the middle and built their cooking fires. The men stayed near the wagons, looking for signs that the Indians might attack.

"What do you think William," James asked ?

I don't know James, we have not had a lot of experience with Indians, so it is hard to say," William answered. "One mistake that I can see we made was not hiring someone to guide us through these parts. Someone who has some understanding of these Indians, I mean," William continued.

"Well, let's keep a watch tonight," James said. "It only makes since that if the Indians do come in, they are probably of the mind to take a horse or two or one of the women. Unless, that is, there are more Indian out there than we can see from here," James said.

"James, I have a good idea," William said in a whisper.

"What," James said impatiently.

"Let's put one of our ugliest women out front so the Indians can see that they don't really want one of them," William said.

"William, that's not funny," James scolded.

"Yep, you're right again James, besides, that would be a good way to lose a couple of horses," William kept on.

"That's not funny either, William!" James said. "Well maybe a tad bit funny," James said, as he walked off shaking his head.

They finished the night without incident. Every one had been instructed to stay within the circle. If they needed to go outside of the circle, they should not go alone.

At day break they pulled out of the circle, with James, Mary and William in the lead. "It would have been nice if we would have had a map of sorts to follow," William said to James.

"You know, I was thinking about what you said about the guide and I think that is a good idea. Let's inquire when we get into Winchester," James said.

"Well, at least you think that I have some good ideas," William responded.

"When did I say that you didn't, William," James asked?

"Last night, my idea of putting an ugly woman out there," William said, laughing and unable to keep a straight face.

"T'is the jewel that can't be got that is the most beautiful," William finished.

That sent James away, shaking his head as he left.

This was not to be a good day. It rained and rained some more. They were forced to pull their wagons up off of the road in deep grass on high ground where their wagons would not sink in the muck. The trail was not passable. Most crawled under their wagons or found space within them as they waited the rain out.

William and James had not met many of their party. Mary had been around, but she had the gift of social graces that apparently not been taught to the Thompson brothers. Most of them were from Ulster. They had left before they spent their last shilling trying to stay in a country that could not support them. That is why they had the means to buy a wagon and a team. When all had been purchased, they had spent well over one hundred and fifty English pounds on the wagon, horses and tack and probably another fifty on blankets, clothing, tools and supplies.

Mary said that she had met three families from Ulster. They had all been displaced on their farms by English Anglican families. As James put it, "Let them have it! Ya' can't make a decent living farming for an English land lord anyway."

"Frankly I spend more time thinking about Mother and Father," James said. "They would have been a big help on this trip, and we would have been proud to have them," James said.

"Well, that all is true James, but no one could have been a bigger help than you two have been so far," Mary said. "I don't know' what these people would have done had you two not come along," she continued.

"What were they waiting on," Mary asked?

"They were a'waitin' Moses to come along and part the sea," William declared. They all broke out laughing. The two kids joined with them. The rain continued to pour down. They could barely se the horses tied on a line along the trees.

They ate biscuits that day, and waited out the rain. Night came and the rain finally gave out.

The men had been under the wagons. They had not been out two minutes before one of them hollered, "The horses, they got the horses."

James and William saw that their fear had come true. The horses had been taken.

"OK, let's spread out. Maybe they did not get all of them," James instructed. "Stay together in twos the best that you can," he said.

Within an hour most of the horse had been located and brought back to camp. Only two were missing. "It's a good thing that there were not more of them, or we would have lost a lot more," William said.

"We are but a few miles from York," James said. "Maybe we can make it there by this evening," he said.

Their information had been correct on one item. That was the abundance of large game along the trail. They collected their take of deer and rabbit as they went along. James and William were finally getting used to the heavy rifles. The smoke that they produced as they fired was blinding. The kick distracted the shooter. It kept the shooter from seeing if he had hit anything. First the pain came and by the time the shooter straightened up, the smoke covered their view.

The powder had to be kept dry along with the patch of cloth that they tamped into place. So far, they had been fortunate.

Chapter XIII

The next day they arrived in York, just a few miles beyond the river. Mary took the children to pick up a reload of supplies while James and William intended to find a guide.

They found an inn in the center of town and asked if there were men to hire for the trail. The bar keeper said that there was a man who used to do that kind of work, but he was not sure whether he did it any longer. They met an older gentleman in front of his cabin and asked if he were Mr. John Stewart that they were told about.

"That would be me," the gentleman said.

"The *bar-keep* said that you used to guide people on the trail. We were looking for that kind of help and wondered if you would be interested," James asked.

"I suppose that I would," the old gentleman said. "What were you looking to give me for my time," he asked straight out.

"What ever your rate is," William said. There is a group of twelve other wagons with us and not a one of us has any idea what is ahead for us. We thought it would be worth while to have someone lead us on from her," James said.

"How for are you expecting to go?" he asked.

"We are not sure, of course, but from what we understand we might find land in Botetourt County, in the Carolina territories," James said. "We are off of a ship one month ago, and the folks we are traveling with don't seem to have a better idea than we do about what to avoid and how best to make the trip safely."

"Irish, are ya?" the gentleman asked.

"Yes," William said, "We are Irish. Does it matter way out here too," William asked?

"No, I suppose not, not as long as you have the price of my fee," the old man said.

The old gentleman explained that during the earliest part of the immigration from Philadelphia, many went no further than the Shenandoah Valley, in the Virginia territory. He said that it was taken by farmers early, because of its river bottom rich soil and the pleasant appearance of the area. He said that Shenandoah was no longer available but that there was land in Botetourt County North Carolina that was farmable.

They finally came to an agreement with the old gent. John Stewart, was his name. He would lead them to Botetourt, County for a sum of one English pound a week of travel. It would be payable at the end, minus two pounds that he would need for supplies.

James and William went back to camp and told the group what they had done and what it would cost them.

One man, a Scotsman named Campbell was his name, said, "that seems a little steep to me. Are you sure we could not have done better."

"Well, if he saves some of us from getting ourselves killed because we have no idea what to expect on this trail, it probably is just about the right price," James said.

"That's assuming that it is me and James and his Mrs. that are saved, of course" William said.

There were no other discussion so they went back to their wagon for some super and peace from that bunch. "I don't know what these folks expect, but it is my guess, with the amount of free game walking along this trail, that it is probably still unsettled, and anything could be waiting for us in plenty of places to hide," James said.

"The old boy knows the trail and is willing to do it again, so that is sign to me that he has some idea what's ahead," William followed.

"Didn't father used to tell us about the Campbell Clan in Scotland," William asked.

"He did," James said.

"Seems that they had many clans of folks under their thumb in Scotland" William remembered.

"He said that several clans had issues when the Campbells tried to claim familial lines of smaller clans that were with them for protection. Papa said that the Campbell clan was as powerful as the De Sweynes, where our line comes from," James continued. The problem came when Campbells tried to eliminate the De Sweynes. The McTavish clan chief would have nothing to do with that."

Chapter XIV

In the morning Stewart joined them for coffee while they prepared to leave York.

They drove all day on their way to Gettysburg. Stewart said that it would take them five, maybe six days to reach the next village. The trail was still rough. Stewart explained that this was once, just a path through the woods. The Indians used to travel on foot, so the use of the wagon on the same path caused a lot of problems. "There are no open plains in this part of the colonies," Stewart said. "We just have to take our time and keep our eyes and ears open for trouble."

The path meandered its way down the valley between the two big mountain ranges. James commented that he had never seen a range like this Appalachian. They continued there way slowly, just west of the Blue Ridge Mountains on their way to Gettysburg.

O several occasions they saw Indians standing on hills close enough to be seen but far away enough not to be an issue. The trail in this section of the road was easily seen. It was a path through the forest. All thirteen wagons creaked through the forest as they slowly made their way towards Gettysburg.

"We best take it slow through here," Stewart said, as he pulled up along said the Thompson wagon on his mount. "Hurrying the horses through here would be a big mistake, this road is rough and it would be a good place to hurt you teams.

It was difficult to keep in mind that they were months away from getting to their destination and hurrying would only bring delays replacing wagon parts or nursing an injured horse.

Stewart stayed at the head of the line, keeping the pace he liked for this section.

Mary and Temperance walked alongside a different wagon everyday, making acquaintance with the other families. "Well Mary, what is new with your lady friends this morning," James asked?

"They tire from the slow pace of our progress," she said. "These forests are so dense, that they can not see, and that is making them anxious," she said.

"Well, maybe we can persuade them to focus on our final destination, rather than our progress," James offered. "I figure that we will make it down to Botetourt County, in the Virginia territory before we can begin seeing settlement sites," James said. "That is still about six weeks away, unless we are to risk the loss of wagons and our teams. We will need these teams to clear land for our farms," James continued. "We can not risk that."

"Why don't ya' teach them one of your good ole Irish songs, Mary," James asked. "Maybe that will lighten them up a bit."

Mary began to sing:

"Near Banbridge town, in the County Down
One Morning in July
Down a green came a sweet Colleen
And she smiled as she passed me by.
She looked so sweet from two white feet
To the sheen of her nut-brown hair
Such a coaxing elf, I'd to shake myself
To make sure I was standing there

From Bantry Bay up to Derry Quay
And from Galway to Dublin town
No maid I've seen like the sweet Colleen
That I met in County Down.

AN IRISH MERMAID TALE

As she onward sped I shook my head and I gazed with a feeling rare
And I said, says I, to a passerby
"Who's the maid with the nut-brown hair?"
He smiled at me, and with pride says he,
"That's the gem of Ireland Crown.
She's young Rosie McCann from the banks of the Bann
"She's the star of County Down."
From Bantry Bay up to Derry Quay
And from Galway to Dublin Town
No maid I've seen like the sweet Colleen
That I met in County Down.

I've traveled a bit, but never was hit
Since my roving career began
But fair and square I surrendered there
To the charms of young Rosie Mc Cann.
I'd a heart to let and no tenant yet
Did I meet with in a shawl or gown
But in she went and I asked no rent
From the star of County Down.

From Bantry Bay up to Derry Quay
And from Galway to Dublin Town
No maid I've seen like the sweet Colleen
That I met in County Down.

At the crossroads fair I'll be surely there
And I'll dress in my Sunday clothes
And I'll try sheep's eyes, and delude herring lies
On the heart of the nut-brown rose
No pipe I'll smoke no horse I'll yoke
Though with rust my plow turn brown
Till a smiling bride by my fireside
Sits the star of County Down.

From Bantry Bay up to Derry Quay
And from Galway to Dublin Town
No maid I've seen like the sweet Colleen
That I met in County Down.

Mary and Temperance finished their song without hearing a response from the other ladies. Thomas and Mary Katherine tried to join in on the chorus as best they could, but outside of William, Stewart and James, no one else joined in.

"They must have spent too much time in Scotland," William offered. "We didn't tell them that they can quit fighting border wars with the English. That's the problem.

"I know one, around here we sing it all the time" Stewart said, and before anyone could discourage him, he began

Gather up the pots and old tin pans
The mash, the corn, the barley and the bran

Run like the devil from the excise man
Keep the smoke from rising, Barney
Keep your eyes peeled today
The excise men are on their way
Searching for the mountain tay
In the hills of Connemara.

Swinging to the left, swinging to the right
The excise men will dance all night
Drinkin' up the tay till the broad daylight
In the hills of Connemara.

A gallon for the butcher and a quart for John
And a bottle for poor old Father Tom
Just to help the poor old dear along
In the hills of Connemara.

Stand your ground, for it's too late
The excise men are at the gate.
Glory be to Paddy, but they're drinkin' it straight
In the hills of Connemara.

A gallon for the butcher and a quart for John
And a bottle for poor old Father Tom
Just to help the poor old dear along
In the hills of Connemara
A gallon for the butcher and a quart for John
And a bottle for poor old Father Tom
Just to help the poor old dear along
In the hills of Connemara

Stewart did not look around as he sang his song. "Maybe no one heard that one before," William said. "Me either."

"It's one that the Irish of America made up to sing in theses parts," Stewart said. "The Irish soon learned that they could make their spirits here just like they did in Scotland and Ireland. The only difference is that we use corn instead of barley. It tastes sweeter and is not as dry as Irish whisky," Stewart went on.

Stewart reached into his saddle bag and pulled out a jug. He took a long swig and wiped his mouth with the sleeve of his jacket, and let out an aaaaaagh! The eyes of the whole wagon procession looked upon him.

"Care for a little pull, laddie," Stewart asked William. William reached for the flask and he heard the loud, uuuuhnnn, from brother James.

"Maybe later Stewart, thank you," William said.

"The Irish have made quite a name for themselves all along this trail. When we get to Shenandoah you will see Irish farms, many with their whisky making contraptions out back," Stewart said.

"In Ireland and Scotland, we used whisky and even the barley malt as trading money," William said. "I suspect that they will pick that up here."

"They have William," Stewart said.

"No sooner than they get their barn built to house their horses, they begin work on their still. Even before they build a house for the Misses, they get their still in. It fills the Shenandoah Valley like a fine morning mist," Stewart said.

"Territory organizers threaten to tax them," Stewart said. "….but I don't see it slowin' them down."

"Somethin's got to give here before long, James," Stewart said. "These folks don't want to pay for the land that they claim. The Irish keep pushin' the frontier out where no land companies have had time to organize it into parcels. The Irish, just don't want to pay for the land. They say that it belongs to God. That may be true in the wilderness, but with the territories, they need to pay for what they take. Land companies pay good money sending trail men out to find new settlement territories. Suppose someone has to pay for that or risk their lives settling new land where the Indians still claim it? Irish come off lookin' like a bunch o' cheap drunks…………."

"Anyway, the Irish need to be a little more careful," Stewart concluded.

"Aye," William said, as James looked back over his should at him. "That coming from a bleedin' whisky Scotsman, can you imagine."

"Isn't Stewart the Scottish line of Kings that King James came from," William asked?

"Of course," Stewart said proudly.

"Well then,…………there ya' have it." William said. "Who's a Stewart to tell Irishmen to be careful about what they do," William asked? "Seems that James had enough trouble minding his own lot."

Chapter XV

That evening they circled their wagons and put out watches around the perimeter.

The cooking fires were lit as dusk fell to night. In the center a larger fire was lit. On it, they rigged a spit for the deer that they killed on the trail today. They let, ole Stewart pay watch over that as the rest of the men checked their wagons and harnesses to make sure that they would be ready to go in the morning.

As the women came over to the center fire, where Stewart had his deer sizzling on the amber coals, some one heard a noise and screamed. The men grabbed their rifles and went to where a woman stood in terror as she stared at three Indians standing near her wagon.

"Hold on here, a minute," Stewart hollered. "They're peaceful, let's not make them otherwise," Stewart said as he approached the trio and gave them an arm shake.

Stewart escorted the three of them to the center fire, while everyone else stood back and watched what was to happen.

"They want us to share some of this meat with them," Stewart said.

"Let'em get their own," Campbell hollered.

"We can do that Campbell, but that is not so smart. I'll deal with them if you don't mind."

Stewart drew his knife and peeled off three good size chunks of venison. "Bring me three portions of beans for our friends, here," he ordered."

The beans were brought over on plates by William, who asked," Is that what they wanted, Stewart?"

"Yeah, they must have smelled us roasting the deer and wanted some of it," Stewart said. "They see this as their land, and see us as trespassers. They don't particularly take kindly to foreigners taking their deer. So's best to give them their fill and let them go on."

"Do you know them, Stewart?" James asked.

"Yes I have seen them before and they may not be looking for trouble," Stewart answered.

"As long as we keep moving, we will be fine. They wouldn't take kindly to us stopping here and building a settlement. As long as we are passing through they will not hold us up any," Stewart went on.

"William, you and James come sit with them," Stewart said. The five of them sat away from the heat of the big fire and ate their portions.

"Just don't offer them any whisky," Stewart said. "That is really asking for trouble for us and everyone who follows us."

Temperance sat with Mary near their wagon. She sensed the Indians looking in her direction. One could not take his eyes away from her. Feeling the attention that the brave gave Temperance, she arose from her seat and began walking to the fire. She stopped about half of the way. She stood still for a few moments.

William saw one of the braves elbow another and point towards Temperance. William became uneasy with their attention on his wife and rose from his seat. Temperance looked back at William and shook her head. William sat down.

She stood still. She stared back at the braves trying to finish their meal. One began to rise. He dropped his plate of beans as he looked at Temperance.

Stewart saw Temperance standing in front of the Indians. "She has no business near them," he told James.

"She seems to be able to take care of her self," James answered.

The other two braves put their plates down and left the fire, looking back as the scurried away.

Speaking loud enough for everyone to hear, Stewart said, "Ya' gott'a leave the handling these warriors to me. That is what you're paying me for, so you might as well let me do it.

"If there is no reason to cause a fight with these people, then we should let them come and go in peace," Stewart said to James. "This is their land, and whether you believe that or not is up to you, but I see it their way and there aren't enough of us to want to change that. Until we get to a settlement, this is Indian territory."

There were no more visitors for the evening.

In the morning they packed their camp supplies and began their walk through southern Pennsylvania territory.

The path followed through the dense forest, into valleys and across river beds, making progress slow. There were few settlers in this region. Native Americans still claimed the area of Southern Pennsylvania their. Through the years several treaties were signed to give safe passage to whites on their way to the Carolina territories.

Chapter XVI

The days on the road came and were gone as they made their way through Winchester, Harrisburg, Staunton Settlement, Fincastle and finally into Big Lick, Virginia that was beginning to offer settlers a place to build. It received the name by being the location of a large salt lick that buffalo and deer frequented.

As James and Mary were preparing to move on, in pursuit of a place of their own, Mary gave birth to their son, John Thompson in 1716. Things being as they were, Mary decided that they had moved far enough and was willing to call Botetourt/Augusta County, Virginia home. They found land in the North Farnham area and began the process of clearing their land.

John was a healthy son and full of life from the beginning. Unfortunately the birth was difficult on Mary, but she began a willful effort to improve.

Before William and Temperance left to find their home on the Virginia coastal country they sat by the fire one night. Mary said, "William's mother gave me the Celtic icon before we left Belfast, as I told you. I had no idea how it would help us, and I really did not have enough faith in it. Now that I have seen what you have done for our family, I realize that I should have listened closer to what Mother said about the icon and how that it might serve us in mysterious ways.

"She is a powerful force, Mary," Temperance said. "She finds her way to protect Irish families in strange and unexpected ways. The problem for most Irish women is that they do not put any faith in her power. Without faith, there can be no miracle," Temperance concluded.

"That is true in Christianity and in *Sidhe Lena Gig*," Mary said.

"Temperance, I knew that you were a special force when I first met you. I took to you immediately, because I liked you. I also knew that you were not an ordinary woman," Mary started. "You were there to explain how the doctor may have fallen overboard. You were there when James and I nearly went overboard ourselves, and you helped me out f the scene in Shanty Town. I believe that you may be the power that *Sheela* provided us to oversee our passage."

"I know that I may not be here long," Temperance," Mary continued. I have been ill for some time and I want to depart this world knowing that James and William will be cared for," Mary said.

"That is why I am here," Temperance interrupted. "Leave your faith in me for I am the daughter and the mother of Ireland, and I have come to take our place in the new world with you and your new family. That is the way that Mother Thomson wanted it, and that is the way that it shall be."

Mary listened to those words closely, and repeated them to herself later that night as she thought about her conversation with Temperance. "That is why I am here," she repeated.

William and Temperance left James and Mary and moved onto the Virginia coastal region in south eastern Virginia.

The Buckalews continued on their way with the two youngsters from the café. They had a ready made family and settled in North Carolina when they arrived a few days later.

The Virginia territory was still quite new in 1716. Settlements were at work in the Shenandoah Valley and around the James River. Jamestown was well over a hundred years old and was in full operation.

James sold the Conestoga for two hundred and twenty pounds sterling and put it down towards the land settlement costs.

They kept the four Destrier, German Shire draft horses. They used them later to produce a line of fine animals like these. The Destrier was well suited for the heavy Conestoga wagons. Once used by Knights, as war horses, their huge frame and superb strength were used in Northern

Pennsylvania by immigrants in Germanna. William Penn had them imported to the colonies and used them for draft horses. The Thompson Destriers were Black to Brown with white lower legs and big hairy feet. They would work out well at Glennforest in clearing trees.

James had a nice home built for Mary and John. It sat above a meadow that James was clearing. He said to Mary one day as he sat next to her bed, "I think that I will restart the old Thompson malt and brewing tradition right here. With the Virginia Territory in its current state, whisky currency may be the safest investment, we can do."

Mary did not say anything. She placed her hand on his arm as she had always done when it was time for him to make the right decision on his own. James did not see that she clasped the icon that his mother had given her, in her other hand.

She pulled the linen wrapped object from her gown and handed it to James. "Give this to John's wife when he marries, someday. Your mother gave it to me the night before we left Belfast." She continued on with labor. "She is the one who looked over us on our voyage to Philadelphia and the one who brought Temperance to us," Mary said.

"This will see to the next generations of Thompson's and their mothers in our new home land. She is the essence of the Irish Mother, and it is proper that her power has left Ireland to join us in our new land," she concluded.

"Your mother passed 'her' on to me so that we could be looked upon with protection and good fortune," Mary finished.

"Your mother said that every mother-in-law has passed this power on to her oldest son's wife for generations leading back to Dumbarton. It is not for you, James, and you must not keep it. It is for the next generation of women."

"Yes, dear," James said.

She held a subdued smile and a tear as she closed her eyes for the last time.

James never got over the loss of Mary. She had been with him since they were young. His parents took well to Mary. He buried her on a hill under a tree with a view of their land at Glennforest.

James raised John, into a strong young man who loved the work on the

Thompson farm. Father's corn whisky business kept he and his father tied to the Scot-Irish community the cropped up around them. James planted enough corn to make several batches of distilled whisky from the sour mash that fermented corn produced.

English Officers followed the movement of Scot-Irish immigrants as they moved south. They were always looking for a product to tax and thereby increase their revenue base for the settlements. That certainly included the making of spirits.

Fighting the French away from America settlements was expensive work for the English. Imports were taxed as they arrived in Pennsylvania and the port in Boston. The Irish began making whisky as soon as they arrived. The English were caught between trying to stop the practice all together or allowing it to continue so that it could be taxed.

James and son John ran a good spirit operation from Glennforest as John matured. They had ample oak to fire the still pot. They had developed a method of hiding the smoke from the fire to keep revenuers from locating their stills.

John and James always lit a few fires from stacks of wood cleared from their new fields to disguise the fire at the still. Revenuers would have to be quite lucky to pick the one smoke plume out of the ten or twelve that they had going at the same time. The sweet smell of the fermented corn was much more difficult to smell. It filled the valley air near Glennforest and drifted in the breeze out onto the road.

James and John ran a small whisky operation near the barn which they claimed was their only still. They claimed they made only what they needed for their own use.

James never considered remarrying. His commitment was to his son and this land. He might have had the opportunity if he would have allowed it to happen. After all, he was just twenty one years of age when Mary died. The region continued to grow as families with young single women coming along, but he focused on John and the place that he had built for Mary. He found it difficult to carry on without her and spent many afternoons under the big oak tree, by her grave marker, talking to her and asking for advice raising John.

By 1750 settlers in Virginia were often at odds with British Officers.

John and his father continued with their still which they was located in their barn. English army officers were despised for their practice of roaming the settlements looking for an enterprise to tax.

One morning, a troop of British soldiers met them at the barn as they prepared to feed the stock. "Are you Thompson," the officer asked?

"Yes," said James, "What do you gentlemen need?"

"We understand that you produce alcoholic spirits on your place, and yet you do not report your activity, nor do you pay tax on it," the officer went on.

"I see," said James, "and what do you think it is that we make here other than what we use ourselves."

"Take me to your still," the officer demanded. "We are told that you provide whisky for most of this county, and profit from it" he went on.

"Come see for yourselves, then if that is what you wish," James responded. "I assure you that you are mistaken. We make whisky for our own use," James said as they approached the small copper still, "and we do, on occasion provide a wee taste to our neighbors, but I assure that is all," James concluded.

"Take this still down," the officer commanded. "You are clearly in violation."

"Is that so," James replied? "You have no proof of your claim and have no need to destroy a farmer's private spirit maker."

"Well then," the officer responded," If you claim that as so, we will give you a pass today, but if you continue to make more than you use, you will face time in the stockade and confiscation of your equipment," he concluded.

"Yes sir, thank you sir," James said mockingly.

The troop rode off into the distance. "They have no idea what they are claiming. Their routine is harassment and that is all," James said. Even if they did make us destroy it, we can make another in the shop. That is all part of being a good metal fabricator, my son," James said

Chapter XVII

William and Temperance purchased a horse and small cart from a nearby wagon maker and began their trek to coastal Virginia. They found a peaceful village across the bay from Chincoteague Island. Once called Gingoteague, or "Beautiful Land Across the Water," this location was ideal for Temperance.

William established a small blacksmith shop where he produced oar locks and other iron fittings for boats and ships of the area. They lived in a small cottage next to the shop. William was not a farmer and was happy to work as a metal fabricator. Temperance was just happy to be near the sea where she could sit and watch the shore birds.

Temperance found William to be a strong husband and a good provider. They enjoyed sitting by a fire on the beach.

"Come with me William," she called. She ran across the sand, splashing in the gentle surf. She pulled him into the surf with her and clung to him with her legs wrapped around his back side as he tromped through the hip high surf.

He took her back to the shore and laid her down by the fire. "Get out of those wet pants William," she said as she helped him take them off. "There is no one around," she said, as she pulled him on top of her and gave herself, passionately to his demands.

"This is a beautiful place," she said as she laid her head across his bare, still wet chest. We will be happy here and we will raise a family of beautiful daughters."

"No sons?" he asked.

"No sons," she said. "I have the only man I need, in you. We will have beautiful daughters, and they will bring their husbands to you. They can be your sons."

"As long as they are beautiful like you, and can sing your Irish ballads, I will be happy," William said.

"Temperance, I can not imagine the daughter that your mother had in mind when she named you 'Temperance," William whispered in her ear. "There is little temperate about you. You are passionate, and you live life like you want it all."

"You savage you," she said, as she rolled over on top of him and brought him back to passion's peak. "My mother was a passionate woman too," she said, when they laid still again. "Perhaps she wanted a daughter with a more temperate passion and live a more settled life," she said.

"We will have beautiful daughters," Temperance said. "You have the seed for as many beautiful daughters as we wish. Come, let's rest," she said as they walked back up the path that led to their cottage.

Their first daughter was born in 1753. They named her Margaret, after William's mother. She had Temperance's raven black hair and fair skin. She was of slight build and had a quick mind to go along with her fast feet that propelled her across the sandy beach, near their cottage.

William added two rooms on to their small cottage when he found out that Temperance carried another child in her womb.

In 1754, a second daughter was born. Temperance named her "Sarah," after her own mother. 1755 brought a third daughter that they named "Mary," after James' wife. The birth of the third child did not change Temperance. She was just as lean and beautiful as she was when he first laid eyes upon her on the ship. She never lost her passion for William or for arousing him on the beach, under the stars where they spent their most intimate times together. Even after their daughters were born, they chose to make love out in the open, with the gentle waves lapping at their feet.

In the Fall of 1755, John Thompson married Hannah Waldrum. She was the daughter of neighbor George Waldrum and a good friend of

James. Hannah was a young bride, several years younger than John and they made a handsome pair.

At the small wedding ceremony, held on the Thompson farm, James met George Waldrum. "George," James said, "apparently the British think that we run a large still operation here. I need your help in discouraging that rumor."

"The problem is, James you make the best in the county, and your reputation has reached Richmond and Williamsburg," George said defensively.

"Well, be that as it may George, we need to keep our little secrets about our passion for our whisky to ourselves, before we lose it," James concluded.

Chapter XVIII

As the years passed, James' farm continued to prosper and so did John and wife Hannah. In 1758 Young John Thompson II was born. James was overtaken with the joy of a grandson and found himself reflecting on his mother and father left behind in Ireland and the happiness that this would have brought for them.

James visited Mary's grave, as he often did, under the big oak tree that looked out towards the expanse of Glennforest and the vast meadow that she loved. James told Mary about their new grandson and how proud she would have been. "He is all arms and legs, my dear Mary," he said. "He will be big and strong like his father, and my father, Hugh."

"Mary's grave was surrounded by a hand made, metal fence that he and John fabricated from brass in their shop. It had an arbor gate in the front as if it were an entrance to a garden that she would have liked to visit. Mary had often brought lunch out for James, giving him a break from work in the field. They would sit under the big oak. It had become a favorite spot for them to sit in the shade and stare out onto their farm and the reality of their wish come true.

Inside the gate, there was another space prepared on the site where James would come to rest at the end of his time.

In addition to their thriving whisky making trade that they ran at Glennforest, James and John the gained reputation as skilled metal fabricators. They no longer referred to it as a blacksmith trade because they avoided the tedious work of making horse shoes. They worked with brasses and iron to make fittings. It gave James great pride in seeing John work in the manner of he and William, when their father taught them in County Antrim.

The metal fittings business acted as a small buffer to their whisky trade. George Waldrum had hired a cooper to put oak barrels together for the Thompson whisky production. "It is only a matter of time before the colonies declare independence from the thieving British," James declared. "They are into to everything, as if they have the right to tax every enterprise that the colonies develop."

John also learned the horse business by helping his father and George Waldrum. They bred the Destrier mares with a chestnut stallion that belonged to Mr. Waldrum. George raised a smaller breed, suitable for the smaller carriages being imported from London. The wealthy in Richmond used the Hackney for use on Sundays and social occasions.

Imported carriages were constructed for the street of London and not well suited for the country roads in outlying Virginia counties. George used a farm wagon, with a large set of rear wheels for the roads in the country. It had a seat which sat on top of the wagon box, up front. This design worked much better on country roads and could be depended on to return to the farm with supplies from Richmond.

George was an Irish-Norse immigrant from Dublin. Mr. Waldrum's people had been long time Dublin residents having come from a line of Norwegian Norsemen who built Dublin as a remote outpost from which to strike English Monasteries or other locations that had too much wealth stored up to make a Viking happy.

Mr. Waldrum always told the tale about his father's family coming from the Vysteinssen line of Norse Vikings that produced the original Duke of Normandy after he held King Charles at siege in Paris. In the old days Rolf loved to attack Monasteries. They had immense treasuries of gold and valuables and Monks always took off running when they saw dragon headed ships come ashore.

"They needed to be relieved of their burden," George would say. "Too much wealth should not belong to a churchman," George always said. "Churches should belong to the people, not to a bunch of robed hypocrites." George was not much on "city religion," as he called it.

Country religion was fine for George, but, "when they got too big for their kilts its time to open the gates," as he would put it. George had a few more determined opinions to go along with that one and he did not mind laying them on to anyone who he could get to stand still long enough. It always seemed strange to hear it from a man younger than John himself.

"Well, son, you are nothing if not predictable," James said on John's wedding day. "She is a fine young woman. One that is fit to produce the second generation of American born Thompsons." James gave Hannah a big hug and was happy that John could start his life here, in Virginia

"I have something that Mary gave me before she died, years ago. She said that it was to go to John's wife, and that she alone was to keep it. Mary said that every mother has passed it on to her first son's wife in the Thompson clan since the old days in Dumbarton, Scotland."

Hannah took the linen wrapped object and stuck it in the top of her dress, where Mary had kept it during their voyage to Philadelphia. When she was alone, she took the object from her bosom and held it in her hands. "It must be something important, she thought." In the light of the lamp, by her bed she unwrapped the icon and held it in her hands. "How strange," she thought.

"How strange this is," she repeated in her mind. "It is strange and it is beautiful. It is strange and it is mysterious. It is crude and it is sexual," she continued. It had a little round head, and funny round ears and hands that went below to open her vulva. It was vulgar, but innocent at the same time. "How strange," she repeated, once again.

"That is exactly what it is," she said to her self. "It is power and it is essence. It is sexual and it is functional." Hannah rewrapped it placed it in her dresser, where she would always know where it would be, just as Mary had.

Mary, she thought. "John always said that her mother had a special glow and a sense of power in her place in the family. Her husband always said that she had a level of authority in her relationship with James, that she took naturally and without speaking or interrupting her husband. Maybe she got her sense of place from this icon," she finally thought as she closed the drawer.

It was decided that John and Hannah would continue on with their lives at Glennforest. John was the only son and should, rightly, take over the operation when James grew too old to do it for himself.

One day when they were sitting at a winter fire in their main room, James thought about his mother and father in Belfast and what the generations before them had endured to survive the conditions of the Irish.

James told John and Hannah about the Lady De Sweyne and the McTavish Clan and the generations that followed. James had written the generations since William Thomson in Dumbarton.

"This may not mean that much to you now, sweet lady but someday it should be passed along to John II, and the rest of your sons and daughters," James said. "My father and his father, all told us of our beginnings, and so shall you."

James still worked the farm and had his hand in the horse and whisky business in 1772 and he was pleased with his growing family that had taken over his house on Glennforest. The house soon became loaded to bear with toddlers. He and John had to make an addition to the house so the aging James could have some peace.

John and Hannah now had John II, and Thomas, born in 1765, William in 1766, and James in 1772. Young John Thompson II was fourteen years old and had already shown some skill in metal working. His father or grandfather began to show him the ways of an Irish whisky maker.

One day as they sat on their front porch looking out across Glennforest's acres, a wagon pulled up in front. A couple and two small children were aboard. "Good, evening there, the man called out as he walked towards James.

"My name is John Lochtomay and this is my wife Megan and our children. We made a point to find your place so we could drop in and pay respects to you and your wife," he said. She was especially kind to us on the day that we came off of that dreadful ship in Philadelphia. She gave us good advice, and fortunately we followed it.

The woman came away from the wagon and asked," Is Mary here so that we may thank her for her kindness?"

"No, we all wish that she were," James answered. "We were just reflecting on our early times here in Virginia and I was telling our son, John and his wife Hannah about Philadelphia with Uncle William," James said.

"Pleased to meet you," John said. "I understand that my mother was a caring and giving person. Unfortunately, she passed on several years ago, much to soon."

"Oh, No," Megan Lochtomay said. "She was special women with a lot to give."

"Well, we will not keep you, Mr. Thompson," Megan said. "We wanted to pay our respects as we are passing through."

"We are going onto South Carolina Territory. We settled for a while in Pennsylvania, but found that we wanted more freedom from Pennsylvania politics," John Lochtomay said." "Events in and around Philadelphia are centered on Pennsylvania, Maryland and a few of the other northern territories gaining their independence from England. It causes problems for settlers having to decide whether they side with the English or with the territories. Someday, this will come to a head and we will all have to deal with it, it seems to me," Lochtomay said. "When that happens, we will all take sides and deal with the matter. Until then, most people want to concentrate on doing something productive with their land," Lochtomay concluded.

"What do you think England's view is on this," James asked? "We do not hear a lot of this issue yet, here in Virginia," James continued.

"Well, England is looking for profit from the colonies. They put a lot of investment into Pennsylvania and Jamestown, here in Virginia. They have not seen any return and have completely lost patience with organizers and Territorial Governors. As a result," Lochtomay went on, "they are increasing taxes on everything imported, like tea, and yet they refuse to pay the costs of raising tobacco that colonies harvest and ship to them. In my opinion, Lochtomay said," They view us as dependent colonies, subject to England's wants and needs," he concluded.

"There have been more potato blighted crops in the last few years. The worst was apparently in 1740, that have brought famine to even higher levels," Lochtomay said. "The Irish are arriving at five times the rate that we did earlier. Philadelphia is crowded with Irish gangs, stealing and pilfering, just trying to get meals for their families. No officials seem to be coming up with answers on handling this many people. The English are not helping, but the affect of their issues years ago have finally taken place. The potato famines are just the last among many," Lochtomay said.

"Well," James said," I am sure we will hear more about this. Settlers have worked their way south into the southern Carolina Territories and soon will be in Georgia. Americans will not adhere to England much longer if colonization westward continues," James said. "The Stamp Act of 1765 still has most of Philadelphia and Richmond upset."

"It has cost England a great deal to defend the colonies against the French, but putting taxes on books and papers will not settle well in the southern colonies," Lochtomay said. "Tensions are mounting all along the trail. We stopped and visited with several families on the way. Most do not recognize ties with Philadelphia, in particular and Richmond, Williamsburg down here," Lochtomay went on. "I understand that they repealed the Stamp tax in '66, but most people still harbor a lot of bitterness for the British."

"By the way, Mr. Lochtomay," James said. "You are welcome to stay the night. We have a small apartment in the stable that you are welcome to use to rest this evening," James offered.

"Yes, thank you, Mr. Thompson," Lochtomay answered," We will do that if you do not mind, and are truly sorry to hear about Mrs. Thompson. She was a delightful woman. A lot of people have become calloused in their appreciation for other's issues, but she was concerned and put herself in jeopardy's way to help."

Seeing Lochmaytomy caused James to remember their short time in Philadelphia and Mary's concern over the Irish. He looked out onto his land and passed the big oak tree and Mary's resting place, and thought about the mixture of happiness and anxiety when they first landed in America.

James wondered how his parents had existed through the continuing decline of life in Ireland. He came to no good view of his parent's outcome, and stored away his thoughts for another time. He knew that they had both passed on by know and no longer had the problems of Ireland over their heads.

One day when the men were out in their workshop, Hannah retrieved the icon from her dresser, where it had been all of these years and brought it into the front room. She handed the wrapped icon to Winnifred and said, "This is for you, from me, from James wife Mary and from Mother Margaret from Belfast. It is yours, and yours only, to keep and protect and someday pass it on to your first daughter-in-law."

Winnie removed the linen from the old icon and stared at it for a long moment. "Who is she mother," Winne asked. "She is the mother of Ireland," Hannah said. "She is everything wise and strong. It has been passed down for many generations and she is now yours to hold and cherish."

When the war for independence of America broke out, young John II enlisted in the Virginia Militia. He left his young bride Winnifred Brickey, to the care of his father and mother as he walked off to war. British General Cornwallis was rumored to be near Virginia and General Nathaniel Greene called his militia in preparation for engagements along the Virginia borders.

In the early years of the war, The Virginia Militia met few British regiments to engage. They stood protecting Virginia's border while militias from Delaware, New York and New Jersey fought with the British at the battle of Trenton and others.

John reenlisted as a Private in under Captain David May at eighteen years of age. Virginia required all able bodied men to answer the call to service in the Revolutionary War. They also required all able bodied men to bear arms when outside their home. The Virginia Militia was originally formed in the mid 17th century to fight Indians and French.

John had packed a small bag and his father's musket, powder, shot and the Indian style, and long handled tomahawk that he and his grandfather made in the black smith shop. James fabricated it with iron that he tempered and combined with carbon until the axe head was hardened. The head had a broad axe blade and a hammer head horn on the back side. The handle was made of hickory. They soaked the handle in water, until swollen and drove a steel wedge into the top which splayed the wood and fixed it to the head. To give the axe extra top weight and strength, James took brass and wrapped the upper section of the handle.

"Try the weight, son," James said. "Swing it back and forth and see how it is balanced," John's father said. "They will have bayonets, but I believe that this thing will give you an advantage to knocking their bayonet lunge out of the way. Let's put a leather wrist loop at the end so you can hang it on your back and be able to get to it without looking for it."

"Let's test it son. As long as you do no allow them to get a direct hit on the handle, this aged hickory will be able to handle all glancing blows." James said as he picked up a section of iron gun barrel pipe. James centered up on John's position and began a lunge at his mid section. "Spin and push the bayonet down and away, John," James said. The Iroquois used this tactic often in fighting the redcoats, and it works well. No body was better at close combat than they were."

After a few practice sessions, John could avert the thrust of the bayonet with his tomahawk with ease. "You see, John, you can out maneuver them every time by wielding this thing in one hand as they stand flat footed with their heavy rifle and bayonet taking both of theirs."

Their ways are old and are calculated to invest lives for enemy assets on the battle field. It is the English way of fighting. They line their infantry up directly opposing their enemy. Their whole advantage is that their soldiers are practiced to take so many shots per minute. They are better than most and certainly better at it than farm boys who have no had their training and experience. They figure that it will cost so many infantrymen to take a hill or an enemy position. The trouble is, son, you are an infantryman," he said.

Practice reloading, but learn to save yourself for hand to hand combat. They are not prepared to meet you, son," James said. "They know only to thrust and withdraw, thrust and withdraw." When they thrust, duck and bring your tomahawk across their rifle stock. Then spin under and give them a lump on the head with that hammer. Good luck."

"Thank you both," John said.

He said his goodbyes to his grandfather, mother, father, and younger brothers Thomas, William and James, and walked off towards Williamsburg, where he would meet up with his infantry regiment. The long axe hanging off of his back, at his right shoulder, swung like a pendulum as he walked along.

On the way he was joined by Aaron Smith and later by John Taylor, both young neighbors. They planned on spending their war years together and returning home when the fighting was over. When John stopped to rest, he practiced swinging the axe as his grandfather had showed him. It felt good in his hand, as did his father's Pennsylvania, small bore rifle. He was accurate with it from distances far greater than he would be allowed to aim at the British.

From his experience before, he knew that the British had standard infantry rifles which were not known for accuracy at distances. The smaller bore Pennsylvania rifle was much more accurate and it was much lighter as well. They were commonly used by Virginia country boys for deer hunting.

On the way to Williamsburg they selected their camps with care because they feared meeting British troops in the area. At this point they did not realize that Cromwell had not yet invaded Virginia. The closer they got to Williamsburg, the more young men they encountered going to enlist.

When they thought they were away from homesteads, they practiced their marksmanship. James could regularly hit a man sized target from what he estimated was a two minute walk. From his experience in the militia in 1776 and 1777, he knew that there was no need practicing any further than that because of the way that his commanders lined up the infantry against an opposing British line.

Commanders held infantry fire until they were much closer in order to maximize the impact. James had never been allowed to use his real skills. At home, he could down a deer from a good distance when he went hunting with his grandfather.

John did not tell his companions about his father's, and grandfather's whisky trade and the taxes that they were told to pay for their whisky. The British began to tax everything that colonial workers made for income. Metal goods, saddles and other items were all subject to British colonial tax.

Americans had put up enough with British intrusion. Thompsons had been in America for over fifty years and no longer considered themselves English colonialists. They never really did consider themselves as English subjects from the time that James, Mary and William got off of the ship in 1715, and they certainly did not now, two generations later.

John signed his reenlistment papers in 1780 in Williamsburg under the Command of Captain Henry Pawling. New recruits were everywhere. They were all there to fulfill their requirements of Virginia Militia law and looked forward to plunking a few Englishmen while they were at it.

Chapter XIX

Their first campaign took them down to South Carolina to meet up with the British and Germans. General Horatio Gates had an army comprised of fifteen hundred continental troops and a like number of Virginia Militiamen. There were the 1st and 2nd Regiments of Maryland, a Delaware Regiment and the Virginia Militia. They would be met by the North Carolina Militia once they crossed the border.

As they entered North Carolina they were met by the North Carolina troops as planned, and began their walk to Charleston, the Provincial Capitol of South Carolina.

Major General Clinton had taken over as British-Commander-in-Chief in America from General Howe who had taken troops from battles in New York and marched to Charleston.

Horses and cannon were lost in storms that plagued Howe's progress to Charleston to the point that his army had to be replaced by General Cornwallis after he took Charleston. Cornwallis was left with the task of taking the rest of South Carolina.

This would be the beginning of a series of battles involving John's Virginia Militia and Lord General Cornwallis, an imposing figure and a respected military practitioner from London. Cornwallis was an experienced field General in combat. He knew where to spend the lives of his infantrymen and was not experienced in losing.

On May, 18th, 1780, Cornwallis sent a brigade of foot soldiers and another from the light dragoons in pursuit of an American force commanded by Colonel Burford who were marching towards Charleston.

The Americans were overtaken near Camden near the North Carolina border.

Cornwallis settled in near Camden and used it as his center of operation and supply. In July John's militia crossed the South Carolina border and continued their march towards Camden.

The British were commanded by Lord Rawdon, while Cornwallis returned to Charleston. Rawdon marched north and met General Gates and took a position North East of town, near a creek bed. During the night Rawdon advanced to collide with the Americans, and John's first battle during his second enlistment began.

John's company settled in near two swamp areas, facing Cornwallis and his two brigades. They made preparations to fight. They had the momentary advantage of position. They charged from a wing position against the British troops. As they reached their location, they kneeled in position while the British formed a counter attack onto the American position.

There was little time to form a firing line with the British advance coming on quickly. John got off two rounds before the British collapsed upon his position. The Americans were caught in the dreaded hand to hand battle with the British equipped with Bayonets. Most American militia companies did not have bayonets, having brought their own rifles from home or found themselves without anything but a knife to face English bayonets.

As the line moved over John's position, he reached over his right shoulder and pulled his tomahawk away. In one motion, he planted it in the chest of his first opponent who was caught in surprise, probably thinking that John only had his Pennsylvania rifle as a weapon. The second soldier, in mid run at John quickly turned away, colliding with another Dragoon troop. He saw his comrade fall with a single downward swing of a menacing looking hammer that came out of nowhere.

Another redcoat came at John and lunged with his bayonet. John spun and struck the tomahawk on the bayonet and lifted it away from his body, just as grandfather had instructed him. He ducked under and caught his opponent with his weapon between his legs and then directly on the back.

Lt. Stevens observed some of this action as John cut down one veteran foot soldier after another by maneuvering his weapon to cancel the thrust of bayonets pointed at his midsection, and then spin around to take the redcoat by surprise.

John's Commander called a retreat when he saw his militia being manhandled by a British force better equipped and better trained in hand to hand combat. The British regiments chased the Americans for twenty miles. The American's lost over a thousand troops while the British and Germans lost three hundred. Three American guns were taken along with other valuable stores.

Unable to supply his Army with uniforms and standard military rifles, General Gates was forced to provide training on hand to hand combat on their march towards an engagement with General Tarleton.

The American forces were soundly beaten and it showed on the faces of the troops and officers. It was not that the Americans marksmanship was inferior. It had more to do with fighting skills with bayonets and knives.

Lt. Stevens of John's company had seen John wielding his tomahawk that he somehow pulled out from behind his back and recognized its benefit.

"Private," Stevens called.

"Yes Sir," John replied.

"Step forward and show us that thing that you pulled out in the battle, son," Stevens said. When John reached over his shoulder and pulled the tomahawk from its sling, Stevens said, "Holy Cow, where did you get that thing?"

"My father and my grandfather helped me make it in the shop at home, sir," John replied.

"That is some weapon son," Stevens said. "May I?" he asked as he reached for John's axe hammer. Stevens swung the weapon in a slow circle with his hand through the strap. "Very nice, son. I wish that all of your companions had one of these. This is much better than a bayonet,…. and the way that you can surprise an attacker with that menacing looking thing gives you a clear advantage," Stevens concluded.

"Do you see this, boys?" Stevens asked as he raised John's weapon over his head? "I want you to see this. This weapon gives young Private Thompson an advantage, and he knows how to use it. You did not see him in action with it, because you were otherwise occupied, but he took down five veteran British soldiers with his hammer, here, and three others collapsed in mid run at him when they saw what their comrades just met up with. While I do not expect you all to find one, just like this beauty, but surely there are some blacksmith shops with a supply of double blade woodman's axes around. Take a look at this one, boys. See what you all can come up with," Stevens ordered.

Over the next several weeks, while the militia was held up waiting on their next engagement, there was a run on hand axes in towns and villages around the American field position. Several of John's militia mates found axes and long handled hammers that they purchased and began practicing with. They found that they could divert the lunge of a bayonet with an upward or downward swing of their new weapons. A new confidence in hand to hand combat came into the unit as a result of this improvement.

British soldiers were veterans at close engagement, but they had not run across a weapon like John's since they encountered Indians of the Iroquois Nation in the north.

The battle over the southern colonies had become a bit of a stalemate as neither side of the war had enough troops to take on large groups of opponents. Most of the fighting while John's group held their position, were night raids and guerilla activity. Troops had time to discuss weapons and train in hand to hand combat.

"Blacksmith shops pounded out short handled broad axe heads as fast as they could, and John showed them how the sling worked.

In January they began their march towards a place called "Cowpens." The militia still did not have uniforms and they had not been issued standard military rifles. Many of the boys, like John, from the Virginia back country militia, carried the small caliber, long rifle that had been developed by German gunsmiths in Pennsylvania.

They would be up against Tarleton again. He had a reputation as a ruthless commander. As Tarleton advanced on General Morgan's encampment, the American took a stand near the Broad River. The position John's regiment took was between two hills near an open field in the expectation that Tarleton would make a headlong attack without stopping long enough to devise a strategic plan. John and his company laid in waiting on the British army marching directly between the two groups of American's, just as Morgan had planned.

The Georgia and North Carolina Regiments were in the front with his riflemen just ahead of them. Morgan had no field guns, but his men were rested and ready to fight.

Tarleton marched his force onto the battlefield and attacked immediately when he saw the Americans, in position, waiting for him.

John's Company and a couple others, manned with their rifles cut down Tarleton's leading line and drove them back with accurate fire from American militia groups that looked like a rag-tag bunch of undisciplined and under trained kids. They were, however, very accurate with their small bore Pennsylvania small game, hunting rifles.

As Morgan's riflemen opened fire on the British line, standing tall in their bright, red coat uniforms, taking extra care to aim at the tall epaulette wearing British officers.

John dropped two, remembering their appearance at the farm, when they came to pester his grandfather about his whisky. Officer after officer were dropped from their horse before the Americans withdrew back to the American line.

The British army was confused by the absence of their officers and they scattered back into the larger group held up near the forest line.

Tarleton then sent a troop of his Dragoons after the retreating American riflemen when they were met with a counter attack lead by General Washington and his dragoons. The British were driven back, once more.

As the British attacked with a line of foot soldiers they extended their line and outflanked the American forces which withdrew in good order. In their rush to take over the American position, the British lost cohesion.

The Americans turn and fired on the uncoordinated British advance, depleted of officers, and unable to collect an effort. Washington's forces overwhelmed the British lines as it attacked the rear of the British line.

The British regiment surrendered, leaving only a company of artillery gunners. Tarleton's cavalry refused the order to provide a reserve for the artillery.

John's company took position and eliminated the gunners, one at a time until they were all killed or wounded. Tarleton fled with remnants of his column.

As they recouped in camp that night, the Americans were proud of their victory and in high hopes of continuing another battle like this one. Their marksmanship provided all of the skills that were needed. No hand to hand combat was needed from the militia. Their new axe handles hung from their backs, untested.

"John," Aaron Smith said, I hear that we are to meet the British next in this place, called Guilford. I heard an officer tell another that we were apt meet a good match there." John was five years older than Aaron and most of the other Virginia Militia boys. He had first joined the militia when he was eighteen as well, and understood the anticipation of more hand to hand combat against veteran British troops.

John had not said much about his previous enlistment, five years earlier when battles were being fought in Pennsylvania and New York being fought by General George Washington and his troops.

Bunker Hill, Long Island, Harlem Heights, White Plains, Fort Washington and a few more took place up North without Virginia's involvement. This enlistment was proving much different. They had been involved in two large battles with major elements of the hated British forces and probably had more to come.

He did not think that his unit officers would want him to tell the new recruits more about how they fought battles in the infantry. John was terrified the first time he met face to face with a line of British soldiers, close enough to hit with a rock, let alone a rifle. John remembered the faster, he could reload his rifle the better his chances were of cutting a British soldier down before he got off another shot at him.

He wanted to tell the younger men that like the brief skirmish in Camden, that this was 'eye to eye' contact with the British was dangerous. He thought if he was going to tell them anything, he would say," this is eye to eye fighting. When you meet a Brit's eye, he has met yours, and it was a matter of who could put a bullet in the other before he could put one in you. If you missed, the faster that the rifle could be reloaded and fired again, the better the chances were of staying alive and meeting the next Brit who took aim at you."

The battle at Cowpens was a strange encounter. The Virginia Militia was able to take a stand and use their superior marksmanship. From a lying position, they had a clear view of their opponents.

The Pennsylvania rifles, or Kentucky rifles as they were known later, were generally inaccurate as the British had seen at Cowpens. John remembered how officers lined the infantry up, facing head-on to the British lines where they fired, reloaded and fired again. John could reload fast enough to get off three shots in a minutes time, which was what was expected of him. Other could reload quicker. Those that could not fire three times a minute were at a severe disadvantage.

When an officer saw that the enemy lines had been breached in continual firing at them, they ordered the cavalry to ride in and hack with their swords. That was when the hand axes would come into play.

Some of the Continental soldiers had new guns from the Hopewell Furnace gun shop, but they were in short supply and not available to militia men who carried their own rifles, shot and powder.

John's regiment began preparation for the march into North Carolina and the battle of Guilford, at the Guilford courthouse on March 15, 1781. They marched to Guilford and set up camp north of the village center.

The Brits were camped within sight but out of range on the south side of Guilford. The courthouse was in the middle. The Brits had small artillery that they used in battle. In many cases they used grapeshot as an anti-personnel weapon, but they also could use a ball that could do damage from a longer distance.

The British infantry had on their red coats and headgear of bearskin caps, while the grenadiers had on their tri-corner hats that they were known for. James and the rest of the Americans were still dressed as best they could. They had been promised the blue uniforms of the continental army months before, but had not received them as they settled in north of Guilford. The officers wore their blue uniforms and tri-cornered hats but enlistees wore civilian clothes.

The British Army was lined on the south side of Guilford. The Virginia

Militia, the North Carolina Militia and the Delaware as well as the others were equipped with muskets. General Nathaniel Greene commanded the colonial troops. Cornwallis had been chasing Greene in tough campaigns in South and North Carolina before he attempted to stop them from re-entering Virginia.

As John stood with his regiment, the British began an advance up to a clearing about half of a mile south of the courthouse. The American line formed across the northern edge of the clearing and extended into the heavily wooded areas on each side.

The North Carolina militia, William Washington's legion, Lee's Legion and the Cavalry held the flanks of Cornwallis position.

"You boys, take your line here, Lt. Johnson ordered. James' Virginia Militia lined up three hundred yards back, near the tree line. The second Virginia unit was a similar distance to the rear of the courthouse with Greene's third line and two guns.

With the pressure rising from close quarters as the lines neared each other, Major Morgan had advised Greene to place another line behind the North Carolina, with orders to shoot any militia men who left their post.

"Men, when I give the order, you will line up, shoulder to shoulder, facing enemy lines. Do not fire until the order is given. Take aim and fire as accurately as you can. Reload and fire again until the Cavalry is ordered to advance onto the line. When I give the order, you will advance behind the cavalry with your hand weapons and meet the enemy hand to hand," Lt. Johnson instructed.

"These British, under Cromwell are professional soldiers and you must take them down with the same accuracy in firing and reloading as they have. We will hold the line at all costs. Desertion from your post will be dealt with severity. You follow orders at all times, just as before and expect this fight to be the toughest we have faced yet," he continued.

"That is all. Get your gear and prepare for battle."

John checked his gear and assisted Aaron and John Taylor with theirs. He thought back on Winnie, and wondered how she was doing. Just as he settled into the image of his woman and the peaceful surrounds of Glennforest, he heard, "Keep your mind on what you are doing. If the Brits see you looking down, fumbling with your reload, they might just pick you out as an open target. As soon as you make eye contact with an enemy soldier, raise your rifle and fire. Do not hurry, or you will miss and he will kill you while you are fumbling around reloading," Johnson told them. "Keep your mind clear, pick out an easy target, and let him have it before he does the same to you," Johnson exclaimed!

"These are good soldiers, boys. Do not let them get the best of you. When I give the order, we will follow the cavalry boys into them, and you will get a chance to see how those new head bangers of yours work."

As they lined up facing the Brits who advanced towards them, John opened fire as the order was given, taking down his first target, closest to his position. The British came behind the clearing.

Cornwallis formed his line of three regiments facing the militia's line. John had his rifle ready and fired again at targets out front as they advanced. Bullets whizzed over his head as he saw Aaron nervously reloading for the first time.

The British advanced across the clearing under heavy fire from James' militia. British soldiers fell as they advanced and the Virginia militia continued to fire. Then John's company caught a break. A fence line stopped the British advance as they forced their way through a narrow gate opening, forcing them into a group, their advance throttled by the fence line.

John and Aaron reloaded, Johnson yelled, "shoot them as they try to get through that gate. Shoot them, damn it! Pour it on them boys, pour it on them! Don't let them through that gate, we got them trapped," he yelled. "Pile them up at the gate, so that those behind them cannot get through." Volley after volley poured into the British line. They were in a panic. Their officer yelled at them to enter the gateway, but they hesitated as man after man dropped before he could advance from the gate

The bottle neck slowed their advance and put their numbers in severe jeopardy as John's company fired and fired again until British bodies piled up at the gate opening. Now, no one could get through the gate.

Their numbers fell as John's company fired upon them continually. The enemy's minds were diverted to seeing what was holding up their comrades ahead of them. They took their eyes off of John's company, not firing, as the Virginia company took advantage of their misfortune. The

British officers were yelling at his troops, aggravated and alarmed as they continued to be picked off by shooters who did not seem to miss.

"Their coming over the fence," Johnson hollered. "Don't let them over, force them to the gate, shoot towards the back of the line and force them forward," he yelled. They aimed and fired as the British line slowly tried to climb over the fence, the gate entry no longer passable. Again, their eyes were diverted from John and his fellow Virginians and they cast volley after volley as each line came upon the fence and laid their rifles aside while they tried to climb over.

It was as if the British infantry men were in a trance, they march with their rifles crossed over their chest and leaned their weapons on the fence as the attempted to climb over.

John saw, young Taylor take a ball in the shoulder and he dropped, writhing on the ground. As John reached down to help him, he was booted in the ribs by Lt. Johnson. "Let him lie," Johnson ordered. We can tend to him later. Keep your mind on what you are doing or you will be down there with him."

Then the second line of British riflemen attacked John's company which had just been reinforced with two other companies. The British attacked again, from another direction, the fence line proving too much of an obstacle.

Two additional regiments joined the battered British line, and the Americans were forced to give up ground under the pressure. "Pull back," Johnson ordered. "Prepare to fire as we go," he ordered.

The British line fell upon John's collapsed company as they tried to withdraw. There was no more time for reloading, and John reached for his long handled hatchet and met his first opponent. The shorter British soldier lunged with his bayonet at John's mid-section. John stepped aside of the lunge, knocked the rifle out of his hand and swung up, menacingly at the Brit's head. John spun to his left and took out another with a stroke to a musket and then up as another fell in the same fashion.

Each British soldier was disciplined. Hand to hand combat with an unconventional weapon like John's long handled tomahawk was something that they were unprepared for.

John continued into their line when he heard Johnson holler above the noise,"look out Thompson, behind you, damn it," as John swung around and disarmed another in his two swing maneuver, one to displace the rifle and another at their head. Johnson's excited voice could be heard from behind, "that's it boys, swing those damned, long handled head splitters boys. That's the way boys!"

Lt. Johnson sat atop his mount and fired his pistol at another as he approached John, who took a low profile and spun again, raising the tomahawk swing upward as he made contact.

The second American counter-attack pushed the British back. Cornwallis ordered his two artillery guns to open fire on the confused melee of hand to hand fighting. The gun's grape shot ripped through fighting men on both sides, and cut down soldiers, indiscriminately.

General Tarleton of the British army charged to John's right. The American's turned on the stricken British line and leveled fire until they were forced to retreat. General Nathaniel Greene ordered his withdrawal as the American Army left Cornwallis on the field. British army had been inflicted with enough damage that Greene knew that the battle, for today was over. They would meet again. His numbers would be an advantage over Cornwallis' depleted forces wherever that was to be.

Cornwallis had suffered heavy causalities that could not be replaced. Over five hundred British soldiers lay dead from the heavy fighting. Two hundred and fifty Americans lost their lives in the battle. John Taylor was attended to. John picked him up and carried him to the medical tent after the British left the battle field.

John's company had taken severe losses in the battle as well. This was nothing like his earlier enlistment when they saw little fighting like this and even Cowpens was not as rough as this had been. He had learned to follow his own advice in the heat of battle, attend to yourself first and keep you mind on what you are doing. John knew that he had made a dangerous choice when he took his eye off of the battle when he reached down to aid young Taylor. He had a couple sore ribs to remember that lesson by.

In September of that year, the Virginia Militia joined two New York and two New Jersey regiments with others for the battle for York town. After Cornwallis marched his army into Virginia and took Yorktown. James' militia marched out of Williamsburg and onto Yorktown on September 28th 1781.

John's ribs and John Taylor's shoulder wound had repaired as they marched towards their next engagement in Yorktown.

John's Virginia Militia formed a circle around Cornwallis in Yorktown. The enemy lined up with Cornwallis' diminished regiments. They chose a position with their backs to the York River. They soon found that to be a fatal error. They were encircled with the American militia and Continentals and the York River.

The Americans put the British Army to siege. Cornwallis was waiting on reinforcements from New York when he found that he had put himself in an untenable position. He was backed up against the river and only one direction to escape.

As Cornwallis gave ground, General Washington tightened the noose around the British army.

On October 9, The American's began an artillery bombardment of the British positions. Weakened by his decision to give up ground to the Americans Cornwallis found himself under attack by American and white coated French troops.

Cornwallis then attempted an escape across the York River, but was turned back by a barrage of bullets aiming at his swimming soldiers.

With no where to turn and the lack of planned reinforcements Cornwallis surrendered on October 19th, 1781 and was marched out of town, defeated. There were six thousand British soldiers who surrendered in Yorktown, with over two hundred pieces of artillery captured as well. Eighty Americans and two hundred French were killed during the siege.

John, John Taylor and young Aaron Smith went through several other battles until the British finally surrendered. They walked back to their homes and were met by their families with relief.

Following the war, John Thompson returned to his wife, and Glennforest. In 1782, Elizabeth was born.

For the time being John settled back into his farm job, helping with the stock, and the metal smith business. They also began a larger production of their corn whisky. People sought good whisky and no one in the area did it better than Thompson. The new oak barrels were used to store whisky, which no longer needed to be hidden in the nearby oak forest.

Chapter XX

As the years passed, William and Temperance and their three daughters stayed on in their cottage, across the bay from Chincoteague Island. The island, and the shore on the mainland, began to change as more settlers came to find paradise in the small fishing village that developed around the Thompson's place. They still had a few acres surrounding their home, but they had to give-up love making on the shore that had become home to other families.

Their passion for each other never quieted. They found each other in the dark of their cottage at night and caressed with the sound of the ebb and flow of the gentle waves, washing ashore.

The three daughters matured. They all looked like Temperance. They grew to be beautiful, raven haired women that loved their life near the ocean. Temperance had to intervene when they were in their teens. They loved to swim nude in the surf near their home. When they were small, they always disrobed before they waded in. It was usually after dark and there was no one who could object. The girls grew up thinking that this was natural. They found nothing strange about playing in the surf without their clothes. No one was around to make them feel guilty.

Other settlers would have had a fit had they known what was going on. No decent Christian would allow their daughters to frolic on the beach in the nude. That would have been strictly forbidden.

Neither the girls nor Temperance ever discussed the fact that the girls still walked down the path from the cottage after sun set, disrobed and swam in the warm summer surf. Temperance knew that they would continue the practice, but she had to make sure that they understood that society would rebel if they came to know of it.

As they grew older, the girls continued to quietly leave the cottage after dark and make their way to the beach. They swam to the rocks off shore and lazily watched the stars of night. They sat with their long black hair trailing down their backs, lying back in the warmth of the summer night.

William worked in his shop from dawn to dusk now. His line of metal fabricated wares kept him busy. He made shutter hinges for the windows of cottages on the shore, wagon and door hinges and other products kept him busy and provided a good living for his family.

The only thing that was absent was James. He often thought of James and his farm.

He knew nothing of how James' son, John, grew up or how Mary faired. William had given into Temperance's wishes to live near the sea. He wanted to do what made her happy, and all things had worked out well for them.

He still missed James and the closeness of the Thompson clan and probably would have chosen to build a house near James' and operated a blacksmith and metal fabrication trade had he had his choice. He did not, and there was no changing that.

The girls were in their twenties when news of a pending war with England reached the Virginia shore. The activity around the nearby port increased as the news spread and the reality of the spoiled relationship with England spread through the colonies.

The three daughters had not shown much interest in men to this point. They seemed content to be with their mother. William knew that she sometimes slipped out with her daughters at night to swim with them near the shore and out near the rocks. He had seen the four of them relaxing in the calm of night.

Temperance combed their long black hair with a sea shell comb that she made for each of them. After Temperance finished with their hair, they leaned back, in all of their innocence and sang Irish ballads that she had taught them. It was a beautiful sound and William drew pleasure from listening to them. He also was concerned that others, who were more aware of the developments around them, might hear them and come to see about it.

William sat watch at night when they were out swimming. He never told Temperance or the girls, but he wanted to make sure that they were safe and that no one tried to approach them.

There were boys who liked to hang around Sarah, Margaret and Mary and William hesitated to think what would happen if they knew that the four of them sat out on the rocks at night, completely nude and without enough modesty to find a way to cover up if they were seen.

William had never discussed such things with Temperance. She was the mother and he let her do what she thought was right for their daughters. He had not given it much thought until they began to look more like young women. Their innocence and naivety fit into the way that the family lived on the shore, but times had brought change to their once ideal life on the shore.

William had seen plenty of activity with the presence of English ships near his home. Something was brewing and he was concerned about James and his son, John.

"John would be about the right age for enlisting in the Virginia militia," he thought. He knew that all men, including himself, were required to carry their rifles with them when they were away from their home, although William had not seen the need for that near his cottage on the shore. There were no French or native Americans to concern oneself with here."

One night while the girls and Temperance were out, he started digging through his trunks to find his muskets and the Pennsylvania rifle that he had purchased in Philadelphia. In the trunk, he saw his old top coat that he wore on the ship. Thinking that he no longer needed the coat he took it from the trunk and laid it across a chair. As he searched through the pockets to see if there was anything there worth keeping, he found the old purple and seal skin hat that he had found that first day on the ship.

"I meant to ask Mary or Temperance about this old hat," he said. "I had forgotten about it and it has been in this coat all of these years. Ha! He said. I will have to show Temperance when she returns." He placed the hat on the kitchen table and went to bed, to read.

Chapter XXI

John Thompson's younger brothers Thomas, William and James began to take on more responsibility around the farm. They learned to clear land and plant crops. When they learned that older brother John was going of to fight the English, they all wanted to join him.

They were all too young to have joined John in the war. It was not for lack of interest since they made John tell them about his battles and how his long handled tomahawk helped him survive the war. John's early memory of his grand father's and grandmother's reception by the English in Philadelphia was all he knew about the English except for those that came to the farm except for those who came to the farm to harass them over the whisky.

As Irishmen continued to arrive in port during the 1700's and 80's eligible men were taken directly off of the ship and enlisted in the continental army. Many did not have to be persuaded much more than to be told that they would be given a rifle and told to kill Englishmen. Irishmen from Shanty Town were even accepted into the forces and sent into battle. All hands were needed to fight the superior forces of the British.

John and other young men of parent and grandparents who immigrated at the beginning of the century and moved down the Pennsylvania Wagon Road, had little contact with the British.

Now, with the British out of the way, colonists thought that they were free to make and sell as much whisky as they wanted.

Thompson's supplied several local inns and families with spirit and was in a position to increase production even further when the new American government decided to discourage the industry.

When General Washington took over the new American government, he listened to the advice of Alexander Hamilton and instituted a Spirit Tax on the production of whisky. This news was almost too much for the Irish, Thompsons included. Taxation had been one of the reasons that the colonies declared independence from England and fought a bloody war to rid themselves of that kind of interference. Now, the new government followed with their own tax.

Hamilton's claim to Washington was to place the tax on spirits under the guise that they needed to increase their treasury following a long and expensive war with England. The Irish were not fooled by this announcement. They knew that the Spirit Tax had more to do with imposing taxes on the Irish than anything else.

They saw that large spirit manufacturers of influence, up north, had encouraged the tax to limit the ability of small time Irish whisky makers. The tax was based on quantities produced in a manner where the larger makers paid very little, while smaller makers had to pay a higher rate.

The Irish had gained such a reputation in the Shanty Towns of Philadelphia and other large settlements that the government gave in to the pressure of religious conservatives that wanted to stop the Irish from making and consuming their own whisky. Not focusing on the moral side of this matter, the Irish saw it as plain and simple discrimination at the hands of their own government. This led to outrage in the colonies by Irishmen from New York to Georgia.

James and Mary had seen this type of oppression in Philadelphia many years ago. The British still had influence over the new government under George Washington.

Washington had an army of spirit revenuers employed to chase down and discourage home made whisky operations. Instead of the British making visits on whisky farms, George Washington had his own enforcers.

The tax rate was too much for Thompson. He decided that rather than giving in, that they would go underground with their production again and let the government spend money trying to find them.

The whisky barrels went back into the forest and the disguise was started again. Decoy fires were lit to confuse the enemy.

Looking to remove himself from the problems with the British and his long war career he wanted to look for land in the Kentucky Territory. Kentucky was beginning to develop settlement land being made available to farmers. He left with wife Winnifred Brickey Thompson (Winnie) and two daughters in the Spring. William, John's younger brother, and his wife, Temperance Brickey decide to move away from Virginia as well.

William's oldest son, James and wife Mary Polly Garten decided to move on to the Ohio territory. They eventually settled in Rush county Indiana where they established a farm in the rolling hills.

John, Winnie, William and Winnie's began their journey to Kentucky pulling a two wheeled cart with their two daughters. They had enough supplies to last the two month walk to Kentucky. John's independent spirit drove them from their home in Virginia where he would have been set for the rest of his life. He opted for the unknown in the Kentucky territory where there were no certainties at all. Kentucky had just been laid out for travel and there were few settlements further than eastern Kentucky when John and Winnie left Glennforest.

In the summer of 1787, they arrived near Lexington, Kentucky. By that time, Winnie had delivered their third daughter, Mary Polly. They found a parcel of land near Lexington and began to build a cabin for themselves and to clear the land for corn production. Kentucky was much safer than it was twenty years prior to their arrival. Native Americans had been bought off and chased from their ancestral lands in the eastern realm of the territory.

Kentucky also became the new center for Irish whisky makers. The government did not have the resources to reach that far into the frontier. Whisky stills became common place.

In order to bring income to the household, while fields were being cleared, John and William began to raise corn to ferment into a sour mash for whisky. They worked hard to clear farm land, but the land was covered in hills and rocky soil that did not make good land for crops.

They had ten acres which had been cleared for farming, along with ten more acres that they would use to produce John's grandfather's recipe for sour mash, corn whisky.

Clearing the land was hard work and it would take years to clear enough trees from the thick forests to produce crops sufficient to bring in income for the family.

Over time, John and William's reputation as a whisky maker took hold. He was after all, the twelfth great grandson of William Thomson of Dumbarton in the highlands of Scotland, along the river Clyde.

William learned to produce a malted stock from barley, for the making of whisky in the Scottish manner. William and his descendants produced enough malt to sell to the established Scotch whisky makers of the highlands in the 14th century.

John's eight great-grandfather was Andrew Thompson of Glasgow. He was the first of the Thompson clan to work full time as a malturer. He provided malt to the larger and long standing whisky houses in Scotland. He was a master at his trade, which had been developed from his ancestors who used malt production as a supplement to their income.

Barley was used in the early days of Thompson fermenting. Corn was an American product but the processing was quite similar. The fermented corn and water were brought to a simmer, sufficient to create steam within the kettle, which condensed and dripped pure alcohol into a container placed beneath the copper pipes.

As a metal smith, John was capable of making his own equipment. With 5 gallons of water, about 20 liters, he included 4 ½ lbs. or 2 kilograms of corn meal and a measure of malted corn grain. Placed under heat this mixture produced a sweet, sour mash Kentucky whisky well suited for pioneer spirit.

Chapter XXII

When Temperance came in with her daughters from their night near the rocks, she quietly looked in on William. He had fallen asleep with a book across his chest. He had a candle burning on the bed side table. "Be quiet girls," she said. "Your father is sound asleep and we don't want to wake him."

When the girls were settled, Temperance went into the kitchen to prepare the coffee pot for William's early morning breakfast. As she put William's empty cup on the table for the morning she saw the purple and seal skin hat on the chair.

She jumped back with fright. "Oh no," she said. "No, not now, please!" she cried.

She went to lie down next to her beloved William, but knew that she could not sleep. The hat stayed on her mind and kept her from peace. She kissed William. He began to stir when she hugged him before going in to see the girls one last time. She kissed each of them before she walked out to the kitchen, picked up her hat and left the cottage.

When William awoke in the morning he saw that Temperance had prepared his coffee cup and had the pot ready to heat on the stove, but he did not see Temperance. The girls were in their beds, still sleeping peacefully.

By the time William rose that morning, Temperance had made her way to the pier in Richmond and secreted herself on board for a return trip to

Ireland. She did not have a cabin on this voyage. She transformed herself to the life of an immortal Mur'uch and form of a mermaid.

She sat at the stern of the ship for much of each day as the ship made its way towards Belfast. No one saw her as she perched above the ship's rudder. Most evenings she climbed on the ship and made her way to a corner near the empty cabins where she spent the night.

As the days passed, Temperance wandered out, away from the ship enjoying her new freedom. She teased sailors aboard her ship by rolling over the waves, causing her audience to whistle and call to her. They had no idea that she was a stow-away.

She had no choice in changing to the underworld. She had found her hat. It held the power that she inherited from Sarah. She did not look back. Destined to return to her lair in Ballyhalbert, and her mother, she moved with urgency.

When she arrived in Ballyhalbert, Temperance took the rock at the entrance of the channel. For days she played with the seals that frolicked among the rocks. She was among her mother's kind and basked in the sun of the late summer. She spent her days relaxing on the rocks near Ballyhalbert.

She was now the beauty that she was meant to be as the daughter of Sarah, Queen Maiden of Irish Mur'uchs. Every detail of her form was intended to work power over men who came to look upon her and lust for her skills. They dreamed of capturing her and bringing her into their mortal lives where they would keep her as a wife.

She watched the sun reflect off of her pearl white skin of her upper body. Her legs and feet formed a long powerful body of a fish and powerful, purple fluke. She could play in the water and swim endlessly with the power of a stroke from her lower body.

She began to tease fisherman as they went by on their way to the pier. She sat upon the rocks and sang her siren songs to test her skills, dreaming of capturing her and bringing her into their lives. Sarah had taught her many of these ballads. She recalled them after some effort and practiced singing them as boats of village fishermen passed.

She had lived with the Thomson family as a mortal woman and had no experience in attracting men as a Mur'uch. Her mother spent little time in preparing her for this. She taught some of her songs and ballads, but Sarah never mentioned how she could attract men or what she was to do with them once she caught them.

When she put her purple and seal skin hat on, it brought the power of the Irish Mur'uch to her. She began to learn the powers and the ways of her kind. Now she just needed practice. She thought that the hat made her look a little silly, but she could not deny the carnal power and image of herself as a female enchantress when she wore it.

Temperance learned to change her appearance as she looked into the eyes of fishermen who came near her. The hat was the difference she knew now. When she wore it fishermen went to extreme to try to take it from her. Some of the village fishermen preferred silk colored hair, while others saw her in red or auburn in her.

One old timer saw her as a plump maiden. His image came from a 16th century fresco that he had seen in a book. She did not like that image of her. She felt bloated and unattractive but the old man loved it.

She had to rescue him from the water one day. She could have taken him below as her first victim, but decided to send him back to his boat and the boisterous crew who almost fell out of the boat themselves while they laughed at the old man making a fool of himself chasing his fat mermaid.

The tale of the old boy would play forever among the lore told at Ned's pub. "Old Bryan Gallagher and his lusty, busty mermaid" they said.

Her whole life had revolved around looking over the Thomson family as commanded by the ancient power, *Sidhe Lena Gig*. She relished the idea of living as an immortal, freeing herself from *Sheela's* oversight. To live as her mother had lived for centuries along the coast of Ireland and Scotland was the vision of her new life.

There were tales of Sarah from Dublin, on Ireland's central east coast to the north of Ireland and across the sea, near Dumbarton on Scotland's west coast and all of the way around to the Hebrides Islands, in Scotland's north. She had lived in those water for centuries and was the mothers of hundreds of sea maidens.

The talk on shore, among Ballyhalbert villagers was about a new beautiful maiden who sang Irish ballads from the rocks, off shore. Some rowed their boats to the rocks to get a better look at the creature. She was as beautiful as any mermaid that had ever taken possession of the rock. She threw kisses at sailors and fishermen alike, as they passed her, while exiting the channel.

Temperance teased them with her beauty and let them leer at her until they came too close. They risked wrecking their dinghies and fishing boats on the rocks to get a better look at the beauty that sat upon them. She would stand, and tease them before she dove into the sea.

Villagers said that she was the most beautiful Mur'uch that they had seen. Their wives spent hours crying and worrying about losing their husbands, and providers, to the new sea maiden.

"She is tall, her fish like lower body, with long and sensuous legs" they said. "Her hair is raven black," one told O'Malley at Ned's. "She has the power to change her form and detail of her body to meet a sailor's vision of an ideal woman."

Stephen O'Day said that she was blonde, others have said that her hair was red and her skin was pearl pink. Johnston said that her breasts were huge, but O'Day said that her breasts were young and perky like a twenty year old. Old Gallagher said that she was plump and robust with a large "comfortable, winter night rump."

"It does not matter," O'Malley yelled, interrupting the loud banter that took place, describing everyone's vision. "Her appearance here will lead to bad times around Ballyhalbert," O'Malley said. "She is not the one called 'Sarah', Queen Maiden of Ballyhalbert. Sarah will come to reclaim her domain. Mark my words," O'Malley said. "Stay away from the new Mur'uch. She will meet her match in Sarah."

The crowd quieted in deference to Old O'Malley. He was the patriarch of Ballyhalbert and was often sought after to help Ballyhalbert through times of hardship.

They stayed quiet for another moment, or two before someone started everyone laughing over Gallagher and the sight of him gasping, sinking and nearly drowning before the Mur'uch picked him up and tossed him back into the boat at the feet of his jesters who nearly fell out of the boat themselves, laughing at him.

The crowd carried on for hours arguing about the details of Temperance's appearance. They paid little attention to anything else.

Then until the winds began to pick up in a storm The shutters on the old inn had to be closed to avoid them banging against the side of the building.

It pushed howling winds and sea spray upon the pier and onto Shore Street. It went on all night and into the next day, keeping fisherman on shore. The seas were rough and the wind made fishing impossible.

They all huddled around the fire at Ned's, waiting on the storm to pass. The crowd was much quieter this morning. They began to recall O'Malley's prediction.

Mid morning, Ned's guests heard a disturbing roar that did not come from the wind. With their hands over their ears, they tried to minimize the screeching shrill. "This is as O'Malley predicted," Gallagher said.

Temperance had been sitting on her rock, relishing the wind blown salt air when a sea serpent the height of a main sail suddenly appeared out of the storm. It stepped onto the rock and stood menacingly over her.

"Be gone!" The serpent roared. Its snake like tongue, lashed out as it spoke. "You have trespassed into my domain." It stood over Temperance and swiped at her out with its webbed and clawed hand. She sat, trembling before the monster, not knowing what to do.

Temperance did not know what to do. "Did she have the power to overtake this monster?"

It began to blow even harder as the serpent raised its arms, gathering the power of the winds. It brought waves over the rocks crashing down upon them. Temperance was slammed against the rocks by waves that crested over her and fell upon on her rock.

The serpent stood firm. Two young sea maidens appeared at its feet. They were smaller than herself but showed no fear of the serpent that towered over them. "Be gone," they said with all of the energy that they could gather. "Be gone!" they repeated.

"Leave my domain!" the serpent roared. The screech that followed was deafening. "Be gone, I tell you." Temperance held her ground, not sure how she could escape this monster that had interrupted the peace of her rocks.

The serpent swung its clawed hand at Temperance. Her face burned and stung as a gash opened on her cheek. She grabbed her face. There was no blood, but she winced at the pain and the power which the monster displayed her anger.

The young mermaids clung to the serpent's legs. It gradually began to transform from a serpent to a beautiful Mur'uch.

"Is this you, mother?" Temperance asked.

"It is I, daughter," she answered. "You should have stayed with the mortals, where I placed you. It was for your good, and at the behest of *Sidhe Lena Gig*, that you lived among the mortals in the new land."

"I have returned to your world, Mother" Temperance said, as she stood. "Why do you attack me? I am your daughter."

"These are my daughters. You have no place in my lair," Sarah said, the front row of her predatory teeth rising out of her mouth like the jaw of a shark rising to take its prey on the surface.

"This is my domain!" she roared! You have no place here," she repeated. "Find your own haven, if you must. Go back to the mortals, but be gone from my realm," Sarah commanded. The roar of her voice, carried across the sea and echoed onto Ballyhalbert.

The young sea maidens sat at Sarah's flukes, undisturbed by the anger that their mother took towards this stranger. They sat back on the rocks, seemingly unconcerned over the disturbance.

"I once lived in this village with you, mother," she said. "I have returned to my homeland to live in your domain."

"Yes," Sarah replied. "You were a mortal child then. Now you have returned to my realm and seek a place in my domain as a sea maiden," she said. "There is but one Queen, here. It is I who rule here. The fishermen of this village are my prey, and that of my young," she said, holding her powerful arms over her young.

Temperance looked at the two young maidens and saw herself, many years before. They were tall, lean and graceful as they sat upon the rocks. They had Sarah's back hair. They mocked Temperance as their mother scolded her.

"Go!" said one. "These mortals are ours."

"Your presence will only bring tragedy and disaster to this village and my daughters," Sarah said.

The young looked at Temperance with contempt and distrust. "These are our shores," the other said.

"Go now. These fishermen are ours and we will not give them up for you."

Sarah crossed her powerful arms in approval of her young daughter's words. They stood with their mother, their eyes as black as coal, and the wind moving their long, silken hair across their faces.

"This will be their domain, daughter," Sarah said, softly. "They will have the fishermen of this village when they are ready. I will return to my place in the north. They will become the wives of these villagers and produce their own daughters.

"You must find your own for there is no future for you hers. There can be but one queen. I do not wish to harm one of my own. Go now and do not return," she commanded.

I was summoned by *Sidhe Lena Gig* to send you to the family of mortals that you joined on your voyage. She asked for you daughter. I do not wish to bring harm to one of her legion. Go now. You will be free to live your life with the family as the great maiden mother intended."

Sarah took the purple and seal skin hat from Temperance's head. "Leave us, and rejoin the mortals," she said softly. "That is where you belong. Go before you raise the anger of *Sidhe Lena Gig,*" and bring her upon all of us.

The villagers gathered in Ned's pub heard the roar and the deafening screech coming from the rocks at the entrance to their harbor. They stopped their activity, but dared not leave the safety of their gathering to investigate the roar that penetrated the clap board walls of their shelter. "What was that?" one asked Ned.

"I don't know," Ned lied. "It is only the wind," he said, busily wiping the counter in front of him.

"There is only one creature in this region to make that sound," O'Malley interjected. "It is the Queen Maiden of the Mur'uch, who has held these shores for millennia. She fights to ward off challengers to her realm," he said. "The 'screech' comes from the mouths of her young."

The others said nothing. Acting like they had not heard O'Malley, they knew that he was the one in this region who knew as much about Mur'uchs and Merrows as any.

O'Malley once kept a Sea Maiden in his cottage, many years ago. They made Ballyhalbert their home. Three daughters were raised. They left the village with their mother many years ago.

Temperance left the rock and began to work her way back to Belfast. She felt the need to return to William and their daughters, if they would have her back.

Chapter XXIII

William had been stunned by Temperance's disappearance. He had no idea where she had gone. He was left with trying to console their daughters over their mother's disappearance.

Despite his best efforts, William could not relieve them. They spent most of their days that followed near the shore, looking out to sea, for her return.

After weeks of sitting alone, waiting for news of Temperance, William began to consider what he would do if she did not return.

After searching for an answer he came to realize that this region was Temperance's, not his. His preference, if he had to live without Temperance, was to return to the area around James' farm and work his metal shop there.

He was not sure what the daughters would think of that but was presumed that they would resist leaving the shore. This was where they were born and they were at home. They were all in their early twenties now. Young men from the region began coming by William's cottage, asking to court his daughters. They were all as striking in appearance as their mother.

Temperance had not taught them much about household matters. Someone would have to take those chores on for themselves, for none of the three knew much about cooking or keeping a house. William knew, however, that the young men who wished to take them as wives would not care about their domestic skills. Their striking looks would secure a good catch. Their difference from their mother was their sultry nature that attracted young men to them. Their outward pursuit of men caused problems in the village among the conservative population.

After Temperance disappeared, the girls paid little attention to anything except keeping an eye on the shore. William was not sure why they looked out to sea for the return of their mother. "Had she not disappeared on land?" William asked himself.

William began to look out over the sea as much as his daughter. He stood on the shore, looking out to see what the girls looked for.

One day, after months of ignoring his business and trying to console his daughters, he saw something swimming far out on the sea. After several minutes he realized that what ever it was, it was swimming towards him. He stood and watched it come closer.

He realized that it was a large creature, unlike anything that he had seen since they left Ireland. It swam with the grace of a seal. Graceful movements of the creature's tail propelled it along like a seal or a mighty fish.

As it neared the beach, he could begin to make out the rough image of a human like form with black hair streaming along its side and down its back as it arched its back and powered its way through the water. Finally, it stood.

William was dreaming. It was Temperance. "This must to be a dream," he said. "What is this before my eyes?" he asked.

She stood waist deep in water. Her torso was unclothed. Her lower half was scaled like a large fish, leading to the large, fish like fluke at the base. As she stood, he saw the graceful curves of her body and knew that it must be Temperance. She had greenish, tan skin below her hips. There appeared to be a long, shallow fin that ran down her back to the base of her butt.

As she worked her way to shore, her flukes disappeared before William's eyes. They were replaced with Temperance's long graceful legs.

She stood naked before him and then dropped to her knees before him.

"William, I have returned from the sea. Will you take me back as your mortal wife? I have returned to live the life that we have had together.

Please take me back," she pleaded. "I was taken back to sea by a power that I could not resist. I have found my way back to you and ask you to take me as your wife, away from the shore where I can live as any other woman."

William took her in his arms and hugged her tightly. She stood naked as she clung to him. William took off his shirt and wrapped it around his wife. "I have waited all of these months for you to return to me. Please come, you are home and your daughters will be delighted to see you," he said.

"Before, we do," Temperance said, "don't you have questions about what I am or where I come from?" she asked.

"Do you not accept me, as I am, without question?" William replied.

He looked upon her face and rubbed a thumb over the scar on her cheek. "What happened, Temperance?" he asked.

"Nothing of importance, William," she answered. "It is a reminder of my place with you and our family."

Temperance put her arm around William's back and hugged him.

Temperance stayed closer to the cottage after her return. They still took their evening walks along the shore. The sea no longer had a pull on Temperance. She was at peace with her past.

Chapter XXIV

In 1789, John's son, William was born. The Thompson farm had come a long way. Whisky making was still their staple income. John made a few other pieces of brewing equipment for his neighbors and others in the region who needed quality brewing pots the trade.

Many whisky makers were making their way towards the new Kentucky territory. Kentucky did not have the taxes of Virginia and whisky makers were able to openly operate their stills without interference from Revenuers or "Do-Gooders."

John held visions of larger crops coming from his farm. He had become calloused to Protestant opposition to whisky making. In the early days, John isolated himself from conservative opinion about his central income source.

As years went on, the Irish instinct for dismissing public opinion had weakened. John had ten children with William coming along is 1789, James and John Jr. in 1794, Nancy in 1795, Sarah in 1798, Thomas in 1804 and Margaret in 1808. He had paid his dues in Virginia and wanted to move on west where the taste of war was less prominent in his mind.

Winnie wanted to be able to visit with her neighbors, but the stigma of a whisky maker's wife was too much for her to bear. With their inability to produce the crops from farming that they wanted, they soon began thinking about taking on land in the new Illinois territory to the north.

Temperance and William began preparations to pack up and head west towards James' place at Glennforest. The three daughters met their mother with a less than warm greeting. William let Temperance handle that situation and aimed at staying out of the discussion. He knew the attraction of the sea to Sarah, Margaret and Mary, and he presumed that they probably would not be happy further inland.

Temperance left the decision up to her daughters. "You may come with us," she had said, "or you may stay here and take over the cottage among yourselves."

"We can not live on land mother," Sarah had said. "We have the same draw to the sea as you had," she went on. "As for my self, I will stay here and make a home with a husband. My sisters may do as they please," she concluded.

Sarah had courted by a young lieutenant from the Virginia Militia that had shown more than a passing interest in her. Margaret and Mary had their eyes on their own suitors and had no intention of living on a farm, away from shore.

William and Temperance finished their packing and began their journey west in a wagon that they had purchased in town. Their trip took one week before they arrived on James' doorstep at Glennforest.

James and William had not seen each other in nearly twenty-five years. They both showed their age, but were happy to see each other once again.

James was quickly taken aback by the appearance of Temperance. She did not appear to have aged more than a few years since James had seen her last. She was still slim and shapely and carried herself in the stately manner that James remembered from years ago.

After James caught William and Temperance up on Mary's passing years before, the trouble with the revenuers, John's service in the Virginia Militia and the grandchildren, James finally asked, "So what are your plans William?"

"We operated a metal smith shop on the coast. My mind is to return to that trade, with you, if you are interested and settle here," William answered. "With your permission, of course, big brother," he answered.

"Oh, there is plenty of call for that trade here brother," James said. "We have more customers now than I can handle and I would be pleased to share it with you. "John and Winnifred are looking to move out west to the Kentucky territory, and beyond, perhaps," James went on. "I would be pleased to see to my winter years with you, little brother."

William and Temperance never fully discussed their daughters with James. He figured that he would be told when he needed to be, if there was something to be said.

In the Spring, John, Winnie and their ten children began their trail towards the Illinois territory. They pulled their two wheeled cart, partly loaded with the essentials of the household and walked towards Kentucky.

Before they left, Winnie took the linen cover icon from her dresser drawer and unwrapped it from the aging fabric that kept her out of sight. Winnie, rubber the figures face, rewrapped it in the linen and squeezed it between her breasts. "Down there, where even Irish freckles don't go," she said, smiling at the memory of Hannah tale about Mary Towes Thompson, many years ago.

The walk was difficult over rough ground on the way to Wood River, the Illinois frontier settlement that was the jumping off point to travel north or, on across the Mississippi through Missouri.

Sarah Thompson married her Virginia Lieutenant and built a mansion on the old Thompson place, next to the cottage that William built for Temperance. When their new place was complete, and Sarah's sisters had moved on, they tore the old place down and settled down to raise three raven haired daughters with stark black eyes.

Margaret and Mary did not marry right away and were not seen near the old place on the shore across from Chincoteague Island. It was rumored locally, that there were two sea maidens who often sat upon the rocks off from shore nearby.

Land in Illinois was becoming available north of Fort Wood River, on the eastern bank of the Mississippi. From there, they would walk north until they found good farm land on the Illinois prairie, in the Illinois River Valley.

John, was commissioned a Captain in The Black Hawk War of Illinois. The war ended with contentious treaties that resulted in pushing Black Hawk and his people out of Greene County, making the development of large acre farms in the area safe.

Once the war ended, farmers flooded in and cleared land near Wilmington (now Patterson), Barrow, Wrights (then Wrightsville), Roodhouse, Athensville and the surrounding area, they soon found that they could operate farms of hundreds of acres instead of ten to twelve acres that they ran previously in Kentucky and Tennessee.

The small villages of Northern Greene County spread out through the county as independent communities in the midst of large tracts of tillable farmland. They brought logistical issues that the nation had never faced before. Before mechanization, these early farms were operated with plows and horse teams. The need to collect corn from the field and transport it with wagon and team and return to the field for another load, necessitated grist mills, elevators and a host of other support trades being located within a short wagon ride from the fields themselves. As this occurred, people found work in Wrights and Barrow and the others, running gristmills, maintaining plows, operating blacksmith shops, hardware shops, grocers, inns and running grain elevators, and so on.

This had never been experienced before anywhere along the Scot Irish Trail. These little communities had to operated independently. Without them, farmers would have to haul their crops to Alton or another city for processing. With the thousands of bushels of grain coming out of these farms, that arrangement would not work.

Greene County, Illinois, with its rich, Illinois River bottom black soil soon became home to independent and large scale farm operations. Until the railroads were developed with stops in each of these villages to collect grain and transport it to St. Louis, Minneapolis and other cities beyond, Greene County was the beginning of what became the mid west's grain belt.

According to *A History of Morgan County*, 1879 Donnelly Publishing, Chicago, John found a quarry of clay, south of his homestead. He collected and used the clay for bricks in the fire place of their small cabin. The early use of White Hall clay deposits along with the rich farmlands became the foundation of White Hall, Roodhouse and Northern Greene County

He had seen bricks used this was in Philadelphia and Richmond for fireplaces and buildings during the war and wondered about the feasibility of building a home out of the clay bricks on the prairie. The clay was a light gray color and fired well in his small kiln that they built next to the cabin. The foundation of the local Baptist church would rest on rows of clay fired bricks with clay from the quarry.

The clay quarry and the manufacturing of stoneware made from it would play an important role in the future of Greene County and future generations of the Thompson family. As the county grew it surrounded the land that settled. A small village prospered between the vast grain fields where churches and shops that became known as White Hall.

Stoneware products from the White Hall quarry would be manufactures and shipped from Minnesota to Texas.

John and his family were early settlers in the area that became Greene County, Illinois. John died in 1843. John was buried on the Doyle farm in nearby Barrow Township. His grave marker read, "John Thompson, Va. Mil. Died 1843.

John and Winnifred's sons and daughters laid roots in Greene County and neighboring Morgan County. Future generations remained in Jacksonville, White Hall, Patterson, Carrollton, Wrights and Athensville. In the beginning, they worked as farm hands, wagon makers and grist mill operators in Barrow, Wrightsville and Wilmington/Patterson.

White Hall became the center for roofing and sewer tile products along with a large variety of stoneware. At the turn of the 20th century, George W. Staples worked the clay quarry in the White Hall as the Superintendent. George's son-in-law, Grover Lee Thompson operated a confectionary and ice cream parlor in downtown White Hall. He graduated from the local business college and took a job as an accountant for the company in the boon years of WHSPS.

The Manager of the Administration Department at WHSPS Co, Grover's immediate supervisor, conducted a competition to design the new company logo for company stoneware that was being shipped by train on new tracks installed in White Hall and neighboring Roodhouse. Grover's design was the map of Illinois as the outline. The logo was adopted as the official logo and put in use on WHSPS Co. products beginning in 1921. It continued to be in use until the factory closed in 1960.

Grover was never given credit for the logo and for some unknown reason, local historians credit the department manager's son. As modern day collection of WHSPS Co. products increase in value, the logo is an important trademark of products produced in Northern Greene County after 1921. The person given credit for the logo was born in 1914 and would have been 7 years old when the logo was first stamped on the thousands of jugs, crocks and hundreds of other products that poured out of White Hall. Grover's sons, James and Edward as well as daughter-in-law Laura Thompson, grand son, Ed and nephew Robert all remember Grover designing the logo.

White Hall remains an important center for early 19th century history for the thousands of Scot-Irish families that first settled on fertile land and valuable clay deposits. Never before had farmers been able to plant hundreds of their owned acres of wheat and corn. Neighboring villages were centered in the wide expanse of farmland where they flourished as independent farm centers into the modern era.

Hugh and Mary's descendants arrived, planted and thrived far from the ports of Philadelphia and Richmond where the Scot-Irish landed and were greeted by signs that read, NO IRISH NEED APPLY.

Thompson Name Origin and Early History

There are several variants of the THOMPSON/Thompson name, however, they all stem from the Northern Highlands of Scotland, near the coast, in an area referred to as Knapdale near the Kintyre loch and Dumbarton.

The origin of the name stems from TAMHAIS, meaning THOMAS. Descendants are MAC TAMHAIS, or SON OF THOMAS. In Gaelic, the MH is "V" so, Mac TAMHAIS is MAC TAVISH. Those that migrated south to England often used Thompson and those who traveled to Ireland often used Thomson.

The highlander use of MAC was often dropped in favor of the *Anglosized* version (Thomson) following the uprisings known as the Jacobite Rebellion. The MacTavishes were, like most highland clans, sympathetic to placing the Stuarts (Stewarts) on the throne. When Charles Edward Stuart, known as Bonnie Prince Charlie" landed on Scottish soils in July of 1745 some highland clans prepared to join him in the fight to gain Scottish independence. The Scottish forces were overtaken by a much larger English army. Sir James took land from many clans, including the MacTavish family. At this time many MacTavishes changed their name to Thomson as it was unhealthy to use the highland preface "Mac".

The head of the modern day MacTavish clan disputes the Campbell claim of MacTavishes as part of their original clan, Campbell of Argyle. He insists that Thompsons predate the union that took place in the 17th century. In this claim, he states that Clan MacTamhais started in the 12th century with the progenitor of all Thompsons, TAUSE who was born in either 1105 or 1106. Tause was the son of Colin MacDwine and the daughter of De Sweyne The Red.

The son of the Colin Mac Dwine and Lady De Sweyne was named Tahmais (or Tavish) and his son became Mc Tavish. Years later it was translated to Thomson and then Thompson by its English spelling.

The land of Dunardry was chartered to the MacTavish clan in the 13th century and remained in their hands until December 1785.

The MacTavish of Dun-Ard Righ

The early years of the 14th century had seen the overthrow of the De Sweynes and their disappearance from Scottish history. They left only the ruins of their castle that bears their name and the records of a marriage of a daughter from the House of Sweyne and Colin MacDuine of Lochow.

The Campbell's who came into Argyle under Alexander The Great were from Perthshire, records show and have always used their own crest, independent of the MacTavish crest. Iver was the brother of Taus and progenitor of MacIver, and then MacIver-Campbells. The Mac Tavish stem from Taus and never took the name of Campbell. This taking the chiefs name was an expression of the old kinship and was a way for the group to promote their solidarity and later became part of the adoption of surnames as opposed to clan names.

This family clan issue between the Campbell's and The MacTavishes seems argumentative and not important. Tracing their roots back to pre-history, it is important and the dispute to genealogists and continues on with modern day clan chiefs.

One of the difficulties inherent in the tracing of family names is caused by the Highland custom of hand-fasting. It was a highland custom of living together as mates for twelve months and a day. If at the end of this time, the woman was impregnated, the union could be held as a binding marriage. If at the end of that time, no child present, either man or woman could simply withdraw from the union and could enter into another hand-fasting arrangement. The custom of marriage and churches ordaining marriages was far off at this point in time.

During the transition between the highland system and the feudal system of the south, this difference of principle often lead to clan disputes. A child, legitimate under the highland system, might not be under the feudal system, and so the clans divided as to the person to whom they should render service.

The Sween girl and Colin must have been married since the two sons, Taus and Iver were legitimate and were the founders of their own clans MacTavish and Campbell.

Thompson Genealogy From the Beginning

William Thompson
B. 1275 Dumbarton, Scotland

Johannes Van Kirk Thompson
B. 1400 Dumbarton Scotland
D. 4/18/1486 Newton Grange, Scotland

Christina Johannes
B. 1449 Scotland.
D. 10/18/1486

John	**1469**
Robert	1470
William	1473
Thomas	1475

John Thompson
Afamsone
B. Drummy LF, Scotland
D. 1526 Fingeralle, Scotland

1. Catharine

B. 1469 Scotland
D. 1494

Andrew	**1490**
William	1492

		2. Elizabeth Gourlow
		B. 1474 Scotland
	John 1495	
Andrew Thompson		**1. Margaret Lochmatomy**
B. 1490 Scotland		B. 1499
D. 1571 Frycayglasgow		
	David 1518	
		2. Isabella Normund
	Thomas 1520	
	James 1520	
	Marion 1520	
	Alice 1528	
James Thompson		**Marion Cochran**
B. 1520 Scotland		B. 1520 Glasgow,
Scotland		
D. 1611 Glasgow		D.
	Thomas 1545	
	John 1547	
	Richard 1550	
Thomas Thompson		**Margaret Henderson**
B. 1545 Glasgow		B. 1548 Glasgow
D. 1587 Syide, Scotland		
	Jacob 1567	
	Patrick 1567	
	William 1570	
	Thomas 1572	

Richard	1573
James	1576

William Thompson
B. 1600 Faichfield, Lananshire, Scotland
D.

Janet Hay
B. 1610 Leith, Scotland

John	1624
Adam	1628
Andrew	1629
William	**1630**
George	1637
Isham	1638
Robert	1642

William Thompson
B. 1630 Lananshire
D. 1687

Mary Fordyce
B. 1638 Clogh, Co. Antrim, Ireland
D. 1657

Thomas	1658
Marian	1659
Hugh	1660

Hugh Thompson
B. 1660 Edinborough, Scotland
D. 1719 Letterkenny, Donegal, Ireland

Margaret Craig
B. 1670 Letterkenny, Donegal, Ireland

James	**1696**
William	1698

James Thompson
B. 1696 Belfast

Mary Towes
B. 1698 Belfast

John I Thompson 1716 - 1786　　　　　**Hannah Waldrum**

John II Thompson　1760　Winnifred Brickey

Elizabeth Thompson   1782 Elizabeth married Jona Williams

Hannah Thompson   1785

>Hannah Thompson - married Israel Strait
Daughter of David Strait and Hannah Briggs.
Hannah is Daughter of Edmund Briggs and
Hannah Ward

Mary Polly Thompson   1787   Mary Polly married Stephen Bridges

William Thompson   1789   William married Roxana Bowen
1886

>Son A   B. 1810 - 1820
Daughter A   B. 1810 – 1820

James Thompson   1794

Nancy Thompson   1795   Nancy married Abel McNail
Abel Mc Nail was a Pvt. In the War of 1812
>In Capt. Shortts Co.

>Raney McNail 1801 Ky.
John A. McNail   1814
Daughter A   1815 – 1820
Caroline J. McNail   1828

John Thompson III   1794 John married Theodocia "Docia" Bandy
both are buried in Thompson-Doyle Cem.

Theodocia was the daughter of Thomas Bandy II
Of Bedford Co. Va. And Cornelia Akers
Thomas Bandy II is the son of Thomas Bandy I and
Nancy Burns

Children

Jameson Bandy   1796   Ky.
Richard Bandy 1797
    Married Angeline Blankenship
    And Elizabeth Roberts
William Bandy 1804
Theodocia Bandy   1800   Tn.
Nancy Bandy   1811   Tn.
James C. Bandy   1815
    Married Elizabeth Capps
    And Lydia Cunningham.

Sally Sarah Thompson 1798 Sarah married William Westbrook
    Of South Hampton Va. Died in 1857
    Litchfield, Macoupin County.

    Children

Thomas T. Westbrook 1828   Il.
Thomas married Nancy Bandy also
Born in 1828 and dies in 1900 in
Ellis County, Texas. Buried in Hines
    Chapel Cem.
John P. Westbrook   1847
William Westbrook   1850   Il.
Horatio "Rash"
Isaac C. Westbrook   1855
Hannah Westbrook   1858

Nancy Westbrook 1860
    Married Ben Ballew
William R. Westbrook 1862
Mary Westbrook 1862
Elihu "Hugh" Westbrook 1873
    Married Minnie Graham

Thomas Thompson 1804
    Married Elizabeth Asher of Tennessee
    Children

    Matilda Thompson 1827
    Cornelia Thompson 1828
        Married William Arteberry
    Louisa Thompson
    John Thompson 1831/32
        Married Lavina J. Atteberry
    Rhoda J. Thompson 1833/34
        Married Samuel Modlin
    Nancy Thompson 1835/36
        Married Samuel Hughes
    James Thompson 1837
    Winifred Thompson 1842/43
    Francis E. Thompson 1845
        Married John Wesley Sutton
    Mary Anne Thompson 1847
        Married William Creasy

Margaret 1808

Thomas 1765 Nancy Anne Mc Neal

    Sarah 1790
    Daughter A 1784
    Daughter B 1784-1794

	John	1784-1794 Capt. John, married Mary Polly Bandy
	James	1784-1794
	Son A	1794-1800
	Son B	1794-1800
	Son C	1800-1810

William   1766   Temperance Brickey

Elizabeth	1791
John	1793
Mary	1794
Hannah	1797
Samuel	1800
James	1801
Susan	1804
Peter	1806

James   1772   Wife and children unknown
Born in Pennsylvania, lived in Ohio

Joseph   1774   Wife and children unknown
Born in Pennsylvania, lived in Ohio

Lewalter Franklin Thompson   **Lucinda Brannon**
B. 1811 Ohio   B. 1819 Kentucky
D. 1847-50 Illinois   D. 1870 Illinois

Oliver P.	1842
John M.	**1844**
Sarah A.	1847

John M. Thompson   Mary J. Smith
B. 1844 Illinois B. 1852 Illinois
D.1873 Illinois

Elias. Franklin Thompson   1869 Illinois
James A.   1873 Illinois

John and Mary were married 29 November 1867 at the home of Elias Doyle's in Wrightsville, Illinois. Ceremony was performed by Justice of the Peace John Doyle. The origin of Elias Franklin's name apparently is from a family friend, Elias Doyle. John worked on the farm of A.G. Smith according to the 1860 Greene County census. John's brother, Oliver, worked on the John Doyle farm nearby. John married Mary Jane Smith, daughter of Allen G. Smith, a farmer in Wrights.

John died at the age of 29 of "consumption" (tuberculosis) and is buried in Hickory Grove Cemetery. Mary married Andrew Cage from Greene County in 1876. They are shown in the 1880 Greene County census under Cage with the James age 7 and Frank (Elias F.) age 12. Mary and Andrew Cage later had a son, Charles C. Cage.

James married Maggie Kerger of Wrightsville on March 9, 1892, witnessed by E.F. Thompson as shown on their marriage license. Maggie was born in Germany, the daughter of Conrad Kerger and Lizzie Wahl. James died May 12, 1899, and was buried at Hickory Grove Cemetery. He was 27 years old. Maggie later married William F. Beebe of Whitehall on August 9, 1901.

Wrightsville was a small township in Greene County in the mid 1800's existing chiefly through the elevator owned and operated by A. J. Wright on the St. Louis and Quincy Line.

The elevator was a 32X80 foot structure operated by a 12 horsepower engine. The silos holding 16,000 bushels of grain. A wagon building and repair shop was also in operation as was a blacksmith shop operated by A.L. Brannan.

Elias Franklin Thompson
Mary Elva Stinnett

B. 1869 B. 1871
D. 1909

D. 1954

Dicey
Grover

Grover Lee Thompson   Jettie B. Staples

James Wesley Thompson

Edward Franklin Thompson

James W. Thompson   **Edward F. Thompson**
Marjorie Ballard   **Laura Mann**

David P. Thompson   Edward L. Thompson
9/9/1942 – 9/16/2006

James W.   Troy
Michael   Carrie

David, was David Patterson Thompson, being
named after Virgina Patterson Ballard's family.

Daniel R. Thompson   Douglas A. Thompson

Christy
Megan   Rebecca
Daniel
John (Deceased at Birth)
Mary Kate Devlin
Thomas James

Carrie
> Ryan Joseph
Courtney Rose

James N. Thompson "Ned"
Joseph "Nick."
Jodie Denise

Judy L. Thompson
Mollie
> Darcy White
> > Carter Cash White
Manda
> Carrington Faith Clark

> Matthew

    The 1850 Greene County Census shows the county divided into two communities, Carrollton and White Hall, plus three regions. The regions were defined by two streams that cross the county from East to west, namely Apple Creek and Macoupin Creek. The resulting regions were "South of Macoupin Creek" and "North of Apple Creek", and "Between Macoupin Creek and Apple Creeks" covering the central portion of the county. Most of the Thompsons in Greene County in 1850 were in this central region, and most of them appear to be closely related to each other.
    One other issue needs further research, and that is the Franklin name in the Thompson family. It has existed at least since Lewalter Franklin Thompson, with Elias Franklin Thompson and Edward Franklin Thompson to follow. A verifiable source is not known, however a reasonable assumption is that Lewalter's father named him after Franklin Doyle.